Praise for

VIETNAM: A WAR ON TWO FRONTS

"Sidney Lens' latest—and sadly, last—book offers reflections on the Vietnam war era on the part of someone who spent a rich and productive life dedicated to peace and justice. His account of the course of opposition to the war will be particularly important to those who aspire to carry on the struggles to which he contributed so much."

—Noam Chomsky

"No one played a more honorable or important role in the antiwar movement, and later in the antinuclear movement, than Sidney Lens. By giving equal attention to the war at home that finally brought the U.S. war in Vietnam to an end—and has more recently kept U.S. combat troops out of Central America—Lens' wise and concise account manages not only to be timely but inspiring."

—Daniel Ellsberg

"The younger generation may not have heard much about the war in Vietnam and the struggle about it in the United States itself, and the older generation may have forgotten much, if they ever learned the truth. This war, which lasted longer than any other U.S. war and caused more U.S. casualties than any other except the Civil War and World War II, was unnecessary and futile. Every person should read this fine book about the Vietnam tragedy, and should vow that the United States will never again get involved in such an immoral effort to use its power to inflict control over the people of a small country."

—Linus Pauling

"Sidney Lens has left us a precious gift for our children's children and future generations to come. He has written an honest and lucid account of how our government became involved in a war of intervention, and why it lost that war; both overseas in Vietnam, against a peasant movement for national independence, and at home, against a popular movement to end that vicious war."

—Sidney Peck

"Sidney Lens' book tells the real truth about our war in Vietnam—clearly, searchingly, honestly. It's all you need to know. That's the way Sid always wrote."

—Benjamin Spock, M.D.

"In the final book of an admirable life as writer-activist, Sidney Lens tells the story of the Vietnam war as he told so many other stories—in clear, spare prose, untangling complexities, coming straight to the moral point. It is all suffused with an understated passion that comes from the fact that Sid Lens was a participant as well as an observer in that momentous time."

—Howard Zinn

BURMA, THAILAND, INDOCHINA, AND MALAYA

BHUTAN

ASSAM

C H I N A

MYANMAR
(Burma)

LAOS

HANOI ✪ • Haiphong

*Gulf of
Tonkin*

VIENTIANE ✪

• Vinh Long

YANGON ✪

VIETNAM

Khe Sanh • • Hue

THAILAND

• Danang
• Hoi An
• Chu Lai

Kontum
• Pleiku

• Quinhon

BANGKOK ✪

CAMBODIA

• Dong Hoi

PHNOM PENH ✪

HO CHI MINH CITY
(Saigon)

*Gulf of
Thailand*

• My Tho
• Can Tho

S O U T H   C H I N A   S E A

A N D A M A N   S E A

KUALA LUMPUR

MALAYSIA

BRUNEI

MALAYSIA

SUMATRA

✪ SINGAPORE

B O R N E O

N
W E
S

I N D O N E S I A

0   250   500
Miles

The dotted line shows where Vietnam was divided between
North and South Vietnam during the war.

VIETNAM
A WAR ON TWO FRONTS

Sidney Lens

LODESTAR BOOKS
DUTTON   NEW YORK

Also by Sidney Lens

THE BOMB

STRIKEMAKERS AND STRIKEBREAKERS

Library of Congress Cataloging-in-Publication Data

Lens, Sidney.
    Vietnam : a war on two fronts / by Sidney Lens.—1st ed.
      p. cm.
    Includes bibliographical references.
    Summary: A history of American involvement in the Vietnam War, including a discussion of the antiwar movement in the United States.
    ISBN 0-525-67320-2
    1. Vietnamese Conflict, 1961–1975—United States—Juvenile literature.
2. Vietnamese Conflict, 1961–1975—Protests movements—United States—Juvenile literature.   [1. Vietnamese Conflict, 1961–1975.]   I. Title.
DS557.7.L46   1990
959.704'3373—dc20   90-5828
                                                         CIP
                                                         AC

Published in the United States by Lodestar Books,
an affiliate of Dutton Children's Books,
a division of Penguin Books USA Inc.

Published simultaneously in Canada by
McClelland & Stewart, Toronto

Editor: Rosemary Brosnan
Designer: Richard Granald, LMD

Printed in the U.S.A.   First Edition
10 9 8 7 6 5 4 3 2 1

This book, his twenty-third and last, is dedicated to the memory of Sidney Lens. It is fitting that the subject matter be Vietnam because he used his talents as theoretician, organizer, writer, and speaker in his opposition to that war.

—Shirley Lens

/

ACKNOWLEDGMENTS

Sidney Lens became too ill even to finish the last chapter of the first draft of this book. It was only with the help of Stuart H. Loory and Erwin Knoll that the book was completed. Stuart Loory wrote the last chapter, and Erwin Knoll edited the manuscript.

Words are inadequate to express my appreciation to them. They were close friends while Sid lived, and they have gone beyond their duty in expressing their feelings for him and kinship with me to take on this momentous task while so busy with their own commitments.

—Shirley Lens

CONTENTS

Photographs appear after pages 26 and 66.

1 THE END

It is the end of April 1975. A long war is drawing to a close.

On the outskirts of Saigon, the capital of South Vietnam, a hundred forty thousand North Vietnamese troops, accompanied by some members of the National Liberation Front (Vietcong), are poised, waiting to enter the city. There is little fighting and virtually no resistance. The president of South Vietnam, Nguyen Van Thieu, America's longtime ally, is holed up in his palace, so demoralized that for hours at a time he refuses to take telephone calls. He is hoping for a miracle: Perhaps the United States will decide to reenter the war. But Lieutenant General Nguyen Van Toan tells him, *"Monsieur le President, la guerre est finie"* (Mr. President, the war is over).

In a television appearance, Thieu speaks bitterly: "The Americans promised us. . . . We trusted them. But they have not given us the aid they promised. The United States . . . is not trustworthy. It is irresponsible."

Back in 1973, President Richard Nixon and his secretary of state, Henry Kissinger, had negotiated a settlement under which the United States would withdraw from the war—after eight years and three hundred fifty thousand American casualties. This agreement called on both the Vietcong and Thieu's Army of the Republic of Vietnam (ARVN) to stay where they were, stop fighting, and try to form a joint government. To strengthen Thieu's hand, Nixon's successor, President Gerald Ford, had ordered that five billion dollars worth of U.S. military equipment—including six hundred fighter-bombers, more than nine hundred helicopters, thousands of tanks and artillery pieces, enough light arms for a force of seven hundred thousand, and complete American bases—be left behind for the ARVN.

But the fighting had not stopped. When the Americans withdrew, Thieu ordered his troops to attack the Vietcong in their base areas, and the Vietcong responded in kind. By early 1975, Thieu's government in South Vietnam and that of another American ally, General Lon Nol in neighboring Cambodia, were suffering one defeat after another. Soon, the setbacks became routs. In mid-March, the United States evacuated its embassy in Phnom Penh, the capital of Cambodia, and on April 17 the Lon Nol regime collapsed as Communist Khmer Rouge forces entered the city.

The situation in Vietnam was just as critical. After Ban Me Thout, a provincial capital in the Central Highlands, fell to the Vietcong, Thieu ordered his forces to retreat. ARVN forces began surrendering by the thousands, and one coastal city after another submitted to the Communists' Provisional Revolutionary Government (PRG). By the end of April, everyone knew that Saigon could not hold out much longer.

On April 27, President Thieu loaded fifteen tons of luggage on a U.S. Air Force C-118 cargo plane and flew off to Taiwan. His career as South Vietnam's chief of state was over. That same week, U.S. jets flew five thousand Americans and Vietnamese allies from Saigon's Tonsonhut Airport to Wake Island, Guam, and other destinations. The American ambassador, Graham Martin, hoped to evacuate one hundred thirty thousand "high risk" Vietnamese—those who had worked for the U.S. military or who had otherwise aided the Americans—as well as more than one thousand Americans and their Vietnamese families. But by the end of April, the airport was under bombardment and could not safely be used. The remaining evacuees would have to be taken by helicopters and small boats to an armada of U.S. aircraft carriers and support ships.

Panic overtook those still waiting to evacuate the country. At the swimming pool on the grounds of the U.S. embassy, thousands waited for evacuation helicopters. Thousands more tried to join them, but U.S. Marines managed, with great difficulty, to shut the gates to the compound. Other marines used their rifle butts to repel desperate Vietnamese trying to scale the embassy walls. In the last eighteen hours of the evacuation, 1,373 Americans and 5,595 Vietnamese were lifted out, and another 65,000 Vietnamese escaped in sampans, fishing boats, barges, and twenty-seven Vietnamese Navy boats headed for the Philippines.

In the midst of this chaos, Ambassador Martin walked three blocks to his home to pack his personal belongings and gather up his poodle. Soon after he was evacuated, the last eleven marines crouched on the flat roof of the embassy, waiting to board the U.S. CH-46 Sea Knight coming to take them away. Their rifles were poised to fend off any unauthorized person who might try to enter the aircraft. When it touched down and they boarded, the long American war in Vietnam was finally over.

A few days after the evacuation, *Newsweek* magazine commented:

> The war has been the saddest chapter in the past century of American history, and it will take years for the United States to come to grips with what it did to Vietnam—and what Vietnam did to America. The faith of Americans in their leadership was practically destroyed and many were left convinced that they had been both seduced and deceived by their government.

What was this long war in Vietnam all about? How did it start? How and why did the United States become involved? Why did we lose?

---

2 THE BEGINNING

The Vietnam War, fought by the United States from 1965 to 1973, was the longest war this country had ever waged. In terms of U.S. casualties—dead and wounded—it took a heavier toll than World War I. Only in World War II and the Civil War did the United States suffer greater human losses.

The Vietnam War was unique in one other respect: It gave rise to the largest and most effective antiwar movement in American history. In a sense, it could be described as two separate wars—one fought with bullets, rifles, tanks, and planes on the battlefields of Vietnam (and of Laos and Cambodia); the other—"the war at home," as it came to be known—fought on the streets and campuses of this country. This second war was waged by young people who burned their draft cards and refused to be inducted into the armed forces, preferring jail or flight to Canada or Sweden. It was also waged by millions of Americans who took to the streets in large and small antiwar demonstrations, who held "teach-ins" at schools to discuss whether the war was justified or immoral, and who demanded in a variety of ways that the United States withdraw its troops from Vietnam.

The resistance at home eventually spilled over into the armed forces. Soldiers and sailors still on active duty formed antiwar groups, established near military installations "GI coffee houses" where they could meet for independent discussions, and published their own newspapers—there were sixty at one time—to express opposition to the very war they were supposed to be fighting. In Vietnam, military discipline sometimes collapsed, and there were incidents when American GIs "fragged" (beat up) their officers—the term came from the fragmentation grenades used in the war—or refused to go into combat. American soldiers deserted in larger numbers than in any previous war.

The war at home was a major factor, perhaps the decisive factor, in forcing President Nixon, on January 27, 1973, to end America's participation in the Vietnam War.

The war that so thoroughly engaged the passions of Americans was, in fact, only a phase of a much longer conflict. It had begun in the 1940s and was rooted in circumstances that reached back to the nineteenth century.

The country we know as Vietnam is an S-shaped area, about three times the size of Ohio, on the eastern edge of a peninsula that runs into the South China Sea. It was originally composed of three regions—Tonkin (North Vietnam), Annam (Central Vietnam), and Cochin China (South Vietnam). France conquered the territory, bit by bit, from 1859 to 1884, and a few years later it merged the Vietnamese regions with Cambodia and Laos to form the French colony of Indochina.

Like most colonial peoples, including the American colonists in 1776, the Vietnamese wanted to free their country from foreign rule and govern it for themselves. In the 1920s, several independence-minded groups joined together to form the Vietnamese Nationalist party, and on February 9, 1930, the party led an uprising sparked by the rebellion of a garrison of Vietnamese troops that France had stationed along the Chinese border. The uprising failed, and the Nationalist party faded from the scene.

A few months later, three Marxist organizations merged to form the Indochinese Communist party. Over the next two years, this revolutionary party organized strikes and peasant revolts aimed at achieving national independence. But these efforts, too, were crushed, and by 1932 the French colonial authorities had arrested about ten thousand Vietnamese dissidents and executed some of the Communists. The leader of this second attempt at independence used the pseudonym Nguyen Ai Quoc; later, he would be known to the world as Ho Chi Minh.

Vietnam languished in colonial dependency until World War II. In 1940, while Nazi Germany was overrunning France, Japanese troops occupied Indochina. In collaboration with a French faction—the Vichy French who supported Germany—the Japanese imposed their rule on Indochina. But the national cry for independence could not be stifled, and it was spurred on by the difficulties the great powers were encountering in the war.

In the famous Atlantic Charter of 1941, President Franklin D. Roosevelt and British Prime Minister Winston Churchill promised "self government" and "sovereign rights" to all people "who have been forcibly deprived of them." Vietnamese nationalists were prepared to make the most of the pledge. A student group at Hanoi University joined with the Socialist party and the Communist party to form the League for the Independence of Vietnam (Vietminh). Its leader was Ho Chi Minh, the Communist fighter who had gained great prestige because of his role in the struggle for independence during the 1930s.

Toward the end of the war, when Japan seized full control of Indochina, a band of ten thousand guerrillas was ready to resist, vowing to smash both "French imperialism and Japanese fascism." Their slogan was "Neither the French nor the Japanese as masters." One or two other guerrilla forces fought the Japanese, but the Vietminh were the strongest, and at this point they had the support of the United States and received arms and supplies from American stockpiles in China. David Schoenbrun, a CBS News correspondent for twenty years, reports in his book *Vietnam: How We Got In,*

How to Get Out that the World War II Office of Strategic Services, predecessor of the U.S. Central Intelligence Agency (CIA), worked "closely with Ho Chi Minh and his partisans."

In 1945, the Vietminh succeeded in liberating six northern provinces, and they established a national government. A million people greeted the new regime in the streets of Hanoi, several hundred thousand in Saigon. Years later, a secret study conducted by the U.S. Department of Defense, the famous Pentagon Papers, acknowledged that "for a few weeks in September 1945, Vietnam was—for the first time in its modern history—free of foreign domination, and united from north to south under Ho Chi Minh."

The new republic issued a Declaration of Independence that began with the words Thomas Jefferson had drafted 169 years earlier for the American republic: "All men are created equal. They are endowed by their Creator with certain inalienable rights, among them Life, Liberty, and the pursuit of Happiness." The Declaration then went on to list grievances against France, much as Jefferson had listed the American colonists' grievances against King George III of Great Britain. Thus was born the Democratic Republic of Vietnam (DRV).

But a wartime agreement among the Allies deprived the DRV of the opportunity to rule the country. Under the terms of this agreement, observed by the United States, Britain, and the Soviet Union, the British were made responsible for "law and order" in the half of Vietnam that fell below the sixteenth parallel. The British allowed the French to rebuild their army and used it, together with Japanese prisoners, to drive the Vietminh forces out of Saigon. Among those appalled by this turn of events was General Douglas MacArthur, the U.S. commander in the Far East. "If there is anything that makes my blood boil," he said, "it is to see our Allies in Indochina . . . deploying Japanese troops to reconquer the little people we promised to liberate."

France was willing to grant the Vietminh a minor role in

governing the country but insisted on retaining French control of the army, currency, economy, and foreign relations. Vietnam would remain a colony in all but name.

The Vietnamese were angry, and tension escalated between the Vietminh and the French. On November 23, 1946, a French cruiser fired on the Vietnamese section of the northern port city of Haiphong, killing more than six thousand people. This was the signal for France to reestablish its power in Indochina and install the discredited former emperor, Bao Dai, as its puppet ruler. Bao Dai had performed the same function for the Japanese during their occupation.

Before long, guerrilla warfare erupted again. General Vo Nguyen Giap, the Vietminh commander, mobilized 70,000 irregulars to fight 166,000 French troops. The guerrillas' great advantage was that they had the support of the people. In 1951, Senator John F. Kennedy wrote, on returning from a tour of the Far East: "In Indochina we have allied ourselves to the desperate effort of a French regime to hang on to the remnants of empire. There is no broad general support of the native Vietnam Government [of Bao Dai] among the people of that area."

By that time, however, the United States and the Soviet Union were engaged in an intense Cold War. France was Washington's ally in the confrontation with the Kremlin, so President Truman and later President Eisenhower gave France full support in the colonial conflict in Southeast Asia. President Roosevelt had promised that France would never again be permitted to rule Indochina, but that promise was forgotten. By 1952, the United States had shipped one hundred thousand tons of supplies to the French forces in Vietnam, and by 1954 it was paying 78 percent of French military costs.

President Eisenhower invoked the so-called domino theory to justify America's role in the war. "You have a row of dominoes set up," he told reporters at a 1954 press conference. "You knock over the first one, and what will happen to the last one is a certainty—it will go over quickly." If Vietnam fell to communism, other countries in Asia would also fall one after another, like dominoes. Vice President Nixon predicted that "if the French withdrew, Indochina would become Communist-dominated within a month."

By May 1954, the French had, in effect, been defeated by the Vietminh. They made their last stand at Dienbienphu, a jungle fortress in northwestern Vietnam, near the Laotian border. Here, 15,094 French troops—5,000 of them severely wounded—were forced to surrender after a long siege. A month earlier, when it was already clear that France faced a debacle, U.S. Secretary of State John Foster Dulles and Admiral Arthur W. Radford, the chairman of the U.S. Joint Chiefs of Staff, had offered to send two hundred American aircraft to bomb the Vietminh surrounding Dienbienphu. But Congressional leaders, including Senator Lyndon B. Johnson, insisted that the United States should take no such drastic action without obtaining the approval of its principal European ally, Great Britain. Britain refused to approve.

At about the same time, Dulles offered to provide France with three nuclear weapons, one to be dropped "near the Chinese border against supply lines," the other two to be used against the Vietminh. This plan, too, was dropped because of Congressional resistance and allied objections.

France had had enough. Its entire empire in Asia and Africa was being shaken by nationalist revolutions, stretching its resources and creating domestic strife. It decided to end the war in Indochina. In April 1954, a peace conference in Geneva was convened by France, Britain, the United States, the Soviet Union, China, and the Democratic Republic of Vietnam headed by Ho Chi Minh, as well as the government recognized by France and headed by Emperor Bao Dai.

In the ensuing agreement, an armistice was signed to stop the fighting, and the country was divided into two zones— one above and one below the seventeenth parallel. The understanding was that elections would be held in both parts of the country in 1956 to reunify the nation under a single government. To assure the Vietnamese that foreign powers would no longer determine the destiny of their country, the final declaration of Geneva prohibited "the introduction into Vietnam of foreign troops and military personnel as well as of all kinds of arms and ammunition." The declaration gave similar assurances to Cambodia and Laos.

The Vietnam War should have ended at this point. But in Washington, the president's National Security Council decided that the Geneva accords were a "disaster." On August 3, 1954, the Eisenhower administration ordered urgent economic and military aid "to maintain a friendly non-Communist South Vietnam" and "to prevent a Communist victory through all-Vietnam elections"—a decision that did not come to light until June 1971, when *The New York Times* began publishing the secret study that became known as the Pentagon Papers.

In the mid-1950s, hardly anyone believed that the Vietminh could be defeated in a free election held in North *or* South Vietnam. A memo by the U.S. Joint Chiefs of Staff that year cited intelligence estimates that "free elections would be attended by almost certain loss of the Associated States [Vietnam, Laos, and Cambodia] to Communist control." A conservative newspaper columnist, Joseph Alsop, wrote that "anywhere from 50 to 70 percent of the southern Indochina villages are subject to Vietminh influence or control. French experts give still higher percentages, between 60 to 90." Leo Cherne, president of the anti-Communist International Rescue Committee, cabled from Vietnam in September 1954, "If free elections were held today, all agree privately Communists would win."

So confident was the Vietminh of its popular support that it gave up to the Saigon government large sections of the Mekong Delta in southern Vietnam, as well as a great stretch between the thirteenth and seventeenth parallels, in exchange for the assurance that elections would be held. A map of Vietnam published at that time by a French expert, Bernard Fall, showed the Vietminh in control of almost all of the northern zone except for a few big cities such as Haiphong and Hanoi, and more than half of South Vietnam, including a large stretch between the thirteenth and seventeenth parallels and a large area in the Mekong Delta.

But the elections were never held. At the urging of the Eisenhower administration, Emperor Bao Dai installed as prime minister a Vietnamese Catholic named Ngo Dinh Diem, who had held administrative posts under the French. In 1950 he had gone to the United States, where he lived in Maryknoll seminaries for two years and managed to impress a number of dignitaries. He was hailed by such conservative anti-Communists as Francis Cardinal Spellman, the Catholic prelate of New York City, as well as by such liberals as senators Mike Mansfield and John F. Kennedy, and even by a socialist, Joseph Buttinger. With their help, and that of a young professor at Michigan State University, Wesley R. Fishel, Diem became a special protégé of the Eisenhower administration.

From this point on, the United States called the tune in Vietnamese affairs. In clear violation of the Geneva accords, President Eisenhower allocated hundreds of millions of dollars to Diem's regime to train his troops and police. By 1956, the United States was contributing $270 million a year to Diem's treasury—more money than it was giving to any other country at that time, except for Korea and Laos. A U.S. military assistance advisory group composed of eight hundred officers was organizing and training the Vietnamese army. A Michigan State University team, headed by Wesley R. Fishel, was reorganizing the police and civil guard.

With all this help, Diem should have been able to consolidate his regime. But Vietnam was a country bedeviled by powerful religious sects and gangster organizations, divided between a strong Catholic minority and the Buddhist majority, and populated largely by peasants who, according to most observers, sympathized with the Vietminh. Because Diem was never able to win the support of the peasants, he turned increasingly to repression as the means of protecting and preserving his regime. Even his strongest supporter, Fishel, admitted later that Diem's policy had been a form of "revolutionary fascism."

In 1955, Diem initiated an anti-Communist denunciation campaign, presumably to reeducate Vietminh supporters. A year later, Diem issued an ordinance giving his government the right to arrest and detain anyone considered "dangerous." This became the legal basis for establishing political prison camps and suspending the right of habeas corpus, which would give an accused person the right to appear before a court or a judge and avoid illegal imprisonment. Those who had fought with the Vietminh were declared outlaws and rounded up for imprisonment.

"This repression," writes Philippe Devillers, a French specialist on Vietnamese affairs, "was in theory aimed at the Communists. In fact, it affected all those . . . who were bold enough to express their disagreement with . . . the ruling oligarchy." Diem's own Ministry of Information acknowledged that 48,250 dissidents were imprisoned under the law. According to Devillers, the campaign may have claimed up to seventy-five thousand lives. Even a semiofficial newspaper, *Tu Do*, protested, "We must have done with arbitrary arrests and imprisonments."

In the face of such repressive measures, tribesmen and former Vietminh fighters retreated to the forests to wage a new guerrilla war. Hundreds of thousands of former Vietminh fighters were still present in the South, and they obtained arms by disarming government troops and police. (Hardly any weapons came in at this time from the North, or from China or the Soviet Union.) After two or three years of guerrilla activity against the Diem regime, the resistance groups united to form the National Liberation Front

(NLF), with a program patterned on that of the Vietminh during World War II. High on its list of objectives were "national independence, democratic freedoms, improvement in the people's living conditions, and peaceful national reunification."

The NLF was not a gentle band of reformers; its guerrillas killed appointed village chiefs they claimed were especially brutal and drove informers and landlords from rural areas, seizing their property. More than three million acres of farmland—about 40 percent of the land capable of being farmed in South Vietnam—was distributed to peasants.

This was especially important because land distribution under the French, and now under Diem, was grossly unequal. According to an American economist, Wolf Ladejinsky, 2.5 percent of the peasants in the South owned half of the cultivable land, while 70 percent owned less than an eighth. The Diem regime was persuaded by U.S. officials to do something about the situation, but its halfhearted reforms provided hardly any relief to the hard-pressed peasants—in large part because the government relied so heavily on the landlords for political support that it couldn't act against them. The NLF, on the other hand, was free from such restraints.

Jerry A. Rose, a former *Time* correspondent, reported late in 1961 that "in one degree or another, 70 to 90 percent of the entire peasant population now leans toward the Vietcong." Vietcong was a derisive name applied to the rebels of the South by their enemies to brand them as Communists, but it stuck. Max Clos, a writer for the conservative French newspaper *Le Figaro*, reported:

> The South Vietnam rice granary is politically controlled by the Vietminh [Vietcong]. . . . The national army of Diem is in exactly the same situation as the French expeditionary corps in 1950, and for exactly the same reasons. It holds the main roadways and the important towns, but the very substance of the country—the men and the rice—have escaped it.

Lacking popular support, the government had to rely on force. It doubled its troop strength from three hundred thousand to six hundred thousand men and instituted a program for controlling the peasantry, the Strategic Hamlet program. Peasants were moved away from their land to fortified villages—presumably to protect them from the Vietcong. Some were many miles from their fields. Even the large amounts of American aid offered to the peasants herded into these barbed wire hamlets could not appease them. As often as not, the Strategic Hamlet program, instead of winning the peasants away from the NLF to the Diem regime, drove them in the opposite direction. And because the Vietnamese so closely identified the United States with what Diem did, they looked on the United States more and more as an occupying colonial power, the successor to the hated French.

By May 1963, even Washington was convinced that Diem could not prevail. In early May, a large number of Buddhist monks and laymen demonstrated at a radio station in Hue, the old imperial capital, protesting an order denying them the right to display Buddhist flags on Buddha's birthday. When the crowds refused to disperse, government troops opened fire, killing nine people. The monks responded by demonstrating in front of the National Assembly, in Saigon, and by going on hunger strikes.

A few weeks later, an elderly Buddhist monk, Thich Quang Duc, seated himself at a main intersection in Saigon, poured gasoline on his robes, and set himself on fire to express his disapproval of Diem's repression. Large protest meetings and six other acts of self-immolation—suicide by fire—followed. On August 21, the Vietnamese Special Forces, headed by Diem's brother, Ngo Dinh Nhu, stormed Buddhist pagodas at Saigon, Hue, and other cities, shooting at random. Thirty monks were wounded, and fourteen hundred monks and sympathizers were carried off to jail.

In October, there were more demonstrations, thousands of additional arrests—this time mostly of students—and many reports of torture. A month later, as the situation continued to deteriorate, a group of generals, with the secret encouragement of the Kennedy administration, overthrew and murdered Diem and took charge of the government. Their first chief, Major General Duong Van "Big" Minh, was in power for only two months before he fell to another coup headed by another major general, Nguyen Khanh. In those two months the National Liberation Front inflicted the highest casualties of the war on the South Vietnamese forces and advanced into the Delta provinces south of Saigon. For all practical purposes, the government was confined to provincial capitals.

By August 1964, the political situation had become so unstable that it was hard to tell who was in power. Buddhists were rioting, and rumors of coups were everywhere. When General Khanh seized the presidency on August 16, he promised a new constitution, but eleven days later "Big" Minh was back in charge, and the constitution promise was withdrawn. Two days later, Khanh quit the government altogether, claiming he had suffered a "mental breakdown." Five days later, he was back in the government as premier. And so it went. During General Maxwell Taylor's brief tenure as U.S. ambassador to Saigon, he dealt with five separate governments.

America's gamble in Vietnam had clearly been lost. The attempt to establish a strong, non-Communist government in South Vietnam was a failure, despite the vast sums of money pumped in by the United States and the fifteen to twenty thousand American "military advisers" who were, by that time, in Indochina. The choice was now either to get out or to get in deeper.

3 A BLANK CHECK

Before the U.S. presidential campaign of 1964, many Americans had never even heard of Vietnam or knew where it was. Some were vaguely aware that their government had been involved for two decades in what formerly had been French Indochina. But Vietnam was ninety-five hundred miles away and seemed about as important as, say, Iran or Guatemala or the Philippines—all places where the United States also had used money and the CIA to help install or prop up conservative regimes. Few foresaw that half a million U.S. troops would soon be fighting in Southeast Asia, that sixty thousand Americans would be killed and three hundred thousand wounded, and that the toll of dead and wounded among the people of Indochina would run into the millions.

But as the 1964 campaign opened, something was clearly going wrong in Vietnam. The reports of "successes" by the U.S.-supported government didn't square with the facts. In 1962, when only eight thousand American "military advisers" were in South Vietnam and the regime of Ngo Dinh Diem had hundreds of thousands of troops fighting the Vietcong, Secretary of Defense Robert S. McNamara had claimed to be "tremendously encouraged" by developments on the battlefront. America, he had said, had "no plan for introducing combat forces into South Vietnam."

A year later, in May 1963, McNamara had again exuded optimism: "The corner has definitely been turned towards victory." Five months later he had predicted that "the major part of the U.S. military task can be completed by the end of 1965," and four months after that—in February 1964—he had announced that "the U.S. hopes to withdraw most of its troops from South Vietnam before the end of 1965." General Paul D. Harkins, who headed the Military Assistance Command in Saigon, spoke in the same vein: "I can safely say that the end of the war is in sight," he said on October 31, 1963, and less than a year later he predicted that victory was "just months away and the reduction of American advisers can begin any time now."

In fact, the war was going poorly for the Diem regime. A U.S. Defense Department study concluded that "only the Vietcong has any real support and influence on a broad base in the countryside." A senior U.S. State Department official told David Halberstam, who was then a reporter for the *New York Times*, in March 1963 that "the thing that bothers me about this Diem government is that the only people who are for it are Americans." Apart from government officials and the Catholic community—which made up only about 10 percent of the Vietnamese population—the regime had little influence.

On the military front, the outlook was bleak. The people's support of the guerrillas gave the Vietcong a tremendous advantage over the government's regular troops. Guerrillas don't wear uniforms and don't rely on heavy weaponry. They can melt into the countryside, hide in the homes of sympathizers in the villages, and strike with surprise. A Defense Department study claimed it would take ten regular soldiers—perhaps fifteen—to cope with one guerrilla. So even though the Vietcong were always outnumbered and outgunned, they kept winning hit-and-run victories.

U.S. officers were frustrated by the Vietcong's tactics. "We wish they would stand up and fight," said the American advisers. Most of the time, the guerrillas preferred to wage their own style of warfare, but on some occasions they did "stand up and fight"—and won, as they did in a village called Al Pac in late 1962. The government's forces, it seemed, were poorly motivated and had no real will to fight.

In an article headlined, "The 'Hot' War U.S. Seems to Be Losing," *U.S. News & World Report* noted that "in spite of its superior equipment, absolute control of the air, and greater manpower, the Vietnamese Army is barely able to hold its own against the tough, wily guerrillas." *Newsweek* reported that "only three out of thirty-five provinces are considered 'safe' by the Diem administration." The *Wall Street Journal* observed that for Diem's forces, this was a "war without will" in which the basic problem was the "reluctance of the South Vietnamese troops to fight." The problem of desertions by Diem's soldiers—including those who went over to the Vietcong—"continues at a high rate in protest against the Diem government," the *Washington Post* reported in December 1962.

The civilian population, particularly in the villages, had little liking for the regime the United States was supporting. "Although the U.S. has poured $2 billion in aid into Vietnam, few social or economic benefits have ever trickled down to the peasants," *Life* magazine observed. Diem and his brother, Ngo Dinh Nhu, responded to the lack of support for their government by intensifying repression. Nguyen-Thai Binh, president of one anti-Communist party, charged that "South Vietnam is full of a hundred concentration camps and political prisons. There are five hundred thousand people in these infamous camps, but a hundred thousand of those imprisoned are anti-Communist nationalists. They dared to defy the Diem rule and now they suffer."

After Diem was overthrown and then murdered, more and more Americans came to realize that Vietnam was not a minor skirmish that would end in a quick victory by "our" side, and Vietnam became an issue in the 1964 presidential campaign. Senator Barry Goldwater, the Republican candidate, urged deeper U.S. intervention, including the use of atomic weapons. "Why can't we make up our minds to win down there?" Goldwater asked. "We never hear the president say we will win, he only says we will contain them." In an interview with *Look* magazine, Goldwater said he would isolate the Vietcong by dropping "a low-yield atomic bomb on the Chinese supply lines in North Vietnam." He also proposed to defoliate the Vietnamese forests to deprive the Vietcong of a place to hide. Such talk alarmed many Americans who remembered how the United States had been bogged down in the Korean War eleven years earlier.

Lyndon Johnson, the Democratic candidate, was just as determined as Goldwater to have the United States impose its will on Vietnam. Behind the scenes, his advisers were discussing various ways of keeping the fragile government of General Khanh from breaking apart—including a bombing attack on North Vietnam and sending American troops to South Vietnam. But in his public statements, Johnson kept reassuring Americans that he wanted and expected no "wider war" and that he was trying to bring home the fifteen thousand or sixteen thousand U.S. advisers—not send in an American combat force.

For those who opposed the war and U.S. intervention in Vietnam, Johnson was the obvious choice over Goldwater, who threatened to commit America to a wider war. Even some young radicals who disliked Johnson because they regarded him as a Texas conservative wore buttons proclaiming, "Part of the Way with LBJ," and voted for him. Johnson's public stance was summed up in a speech he delivered in his home state:

> I have had advice to load our planes with bombs and to drop them on certain areas that I think would enlarge the war and result in our committing a good many American boys to fighting a war I think ought to be fought by the boys of Asia to help protect their own land. And for that reason I haven't chosen to enlarge the war.

The public had no way of knowing that the war had already been enlarged—and would soon be enlarged still more. On February 1, 1964, Johnson had approved Operation Plan 34A, which called for "progressively escalating pressure" on North Vietnam. The United States already was sending U-2 spy planes on clandestine flights over North Vietnam, kidnapping North Vietnamese citizens to obtain intelligence, parachuting sabotage teams into the North, and carrying out commando raids from the sea to blow up bridges, railroad tracks, and coastal installations. In addition, CIA pilots or mercenaries hired in Thailand manned forty T-28 propeller planes and conducted air operations against North Vietnam from Laos. The planes carried Laotian Air Force markings but were owned by America.

These aggressive actions were known to only a few people within the U.S. government; they did not become public knowledge until after a top-secret study by Defense Department scholars—dubbed the Pentagon Papers—was leaked to the *New York Times* seven years later by Daniel Ellsberg, one of the authors of the Pentagon Papers.

More troubling than Operation Plan 34A was a series of events that took place in the Tonkin Gulf during the first days of August 1964, which resulted in giving Johnson a blank check to commit more and more U.S. forces to Vietnam. At that time, too, the full facts were not known by the general public until they were reconstructed years later by journalists I. F. Stone and David Wise, and by Marvin Kalb of NBC News in a special one-hour television documentary aired in 1985.

At about midnight of July 30, 1964, the South Vietnamese Navy—operating under U.S. command—raided two North Vietnamese islands in the Gulf of Tonkin. A U.S. destroyer, the *Maddox*, was in the area at the time. A couple of days later, on August 2, three North Vietnamese PT boats "made a run" at the American destroyer, perhaps mistaking it—according to the Pentagon Papers—"for a South Vietnamese escort vessel." In the engagement that followed, one PT boat was "knocked dead in the water" by the *Maddox*'s five-inch guns, and the other two were damaged by U.S. planes from the aircraft carrier *Ticonderoga*. There were no American casualties.

Two days later, on a dark and overcast night, the *Maddox* and another U.S. destroyer, the *Turner Joy*, were again on patrol in the Tonkin Gulf near North Vietnam. The two destroyers reported that they found themselves "under continuous attack" and that the *Turner Joy* "returned" the fire for four hours. The task force commander, Commodore John J. Herrick, later admitted, however, that the *Turner Joy* had located no enemy torpedoes on its sonar and that all the reports of torpedoes had come from a young sonarman on the *Maddox*. The captain of the *Maddox* concluded that what the sonarman had heard was probably the sound of the ship's own propellers. The following day, Commodore Herrick cabled the Pentagon that "review of action makes many recorded contacts and torpedoes fired appear doubtful. Freak weather effects and overeager sonarman may have accounted for many reports. No actual visual sightings by *Maddox*. Suggest complete evaluation before any further action."

It was four years before this cable came to light. Despite the commodore's request for "complete evaluation before any further action," President Johnson was already acting. In a dramatic appearance on network television just before midnight, Johnson announced that two U.S. destroyers had been "attacked" by North Vietnam and that a retaliatory U.S. air strike had been launched. An oil-storage facility at Vinh, just north of the line dividing North Vietnam from South Vietnam, was destroyed, along with twenty-five PT boats.

The reaction of the press, the public, and Congress was one of overwhelming outrage against North Vietnam. The president's popularity rose immediately from 42 to 72 percent, according to a Harris Poll.

In this tense atmosphere, with a national rally-'round-the-flag mood in full swing, the administration submitted to Congress a resolution it had drafted months earlier and had held for an opportune moment. It was the blank check Johnson wanted, granting the president the power "to take all necessary measures to repel any armed attack against the forces of the United States and to prevent further aggression." The House of Representatives unanimously approved the Tonkin Gulf Resolution, as it came to be known, with only one abstention. In the Senate, two mavericks, Wayne Morse, of Oregon, and Ernest Gruening, of Alaska, cast the only negative votes. Morse insisted that the *Maddox* had been in the territorial waters of North Vietnam supporting a South Vietnamese naval raid.

A number of other senators expressed concern that the president might interpret the Tonkin Gulf Resolution as a blank check. Under Article I, Section 8 of the Constitution, they pointed out, only Congress has the right to declare war. The administration denied that it sought to deprive Congress of its constitutional prerogative and persuaded several reluctant senators to support the resolution. Three years later, however, Under Secretary of State Nicholas Katzenbach vehemently argued at a hearing of the Senate Foreign Relations Committee that the resolution had been the "functional equivalent" of a Congressional declaration of war.

So the Johnson administration drew the United States into a war about which the people and the Congress had been kept uninformed. The final decision to plunge in was made in September 1964 even as the president was proclaiming his intention to keep America out of a "wider" war.

It would be unfair to accuse Johnson of "wanting" the war. He would have preferred to see the National Liberation Front surrender of its own accord and to have South Vietnam become an independent nation aligned with the United States. He believed, at the outset, that he might achieve this result just by bombing North Vietnam; faced with American air might, Ho Chi Minh would force the NLF to give up the fight. But when this didn't work, Johnson did what he had promised the American people he would not do: He sent American "boys" to fight a war in Southeast Asia.

4 A MOST BIZARRE CONFLICT

"The Vietnam war is the most bizarre conflict ever covered by the press," wrote one of the reporters who covered it, Robert C. Miller of United Press International. "There are no fronts, no rear areas or secure sections. Officially, it isn't even a war; historically there is no official date when it started, nor is there a definite objective—like unconditional surrender—required for its finish. There are no campaigns, glorious victories, clear defeats as there were in World Wars I and II and Korea."

Except, perhaps, for the three-and-a-half-year campaign against Emilio Aguinaldo's Filipino nationalists during the Spanish American War at the turn of this century, the United States had never before fought this kind of a war. It was waged by guerrillas whose battle techniques resembled those of the American minutemen of 1776 and who said they were engaged in a "people's war." John F. Kennedy described a "people's war" or "revolutionary war" as "war by ambush instead of by combat; by infiltration instead of aggression, seeking victory by eroding and exhausting the enemy instead of engaging him."

Communist leaders in Vietnam cited four military rules for waging a people's war: (1) When the enemy advances, retreat. (2) When the enemy halts, harass. (3) When the enemy avoids battle, attack. (4) When the enemy retreats, follow. They believed, in other words, that the guerrillas in a people's war must try to be invisible because their adversary has a great advantage in guns and planes and that guerrillas should go on the offensive only when they can mount a surprise attack when all of the circumstances favor them.

Those who fight such a war always require a place to hide, and that means they must have the steady support of the people. In addition to the four military rules, therefore, the Vietcong were to observe six rules of conduct: (1) Take nothing without permission. (2) Never be disorderly. (3) Learn local customs and abide by them. (4) Stay with the poor peasants and help them with their work. (5) Engage in constant propaganda. (6) Form study groups for the peasants and attend their open meetings.

President Johnson knew about guerrillas and their people's wars—how they had succeeded in some places (Algeria, Indonesia, Kenya) and had failed or been forced into a stalemate in others (Malaya, the Philippines). But by the end of 1964, the president felt the only choice he had was to wade deeper into what one song of protest against the war would call the Big Muddy of Vietnam.

On September 7, 1964, a White House strategy meeting reached the consensus that "military actions" in Vietnam were "inevitable." Even Johnson's more optimistic advisers could see that the South Vietnamese government would not be able to hold out much longer on its own. Ambassador Maxwell D. Taylor gave it only "a fifty-fifty chance of lasting out the year." Rioting between Buddhists and Catholics in Saigon had reached such proportions that in just one week, 449 people were killed—either by their antagonists or by government troops trying to "keep order."

It seemed clear that the only way to prevent a Vietcong victory was for the United States to assume a more active role in the war. Two plans were considered—one, to bomb North Vietnam so heavily that Ho Chi Minh would understand that the only way to save his country from total destruction would be to persuade the Vietcong to stop fighting in the South; the second, to dispatch U.S. combat troops to the South if the sustained bombing of North Vietnam didn't do the job. The only major figure among Johnson's advisers who dissented from this consensus was Under Secretary of State George W. Ball, who suggested that the United States could avoid war by negotiating with the other side. If Johnson had heeded this suggestion—which other advisers, too, began offering a year or two later—the United States would have been spared a great deal of trouble, expense, and cost in human lives and domestic disruption.

During the election campaign, the president had promised that he would not "widen" the war. When he did widen it after he won the election, he had to make it appear that he was forced to do so by enemy provocations. On February 7, 1965, Vietcong guerrillas attacked a U.S. air base at Pleiku in the Central Highlands of South Vietnam, killing 8 Americans and wounding 126 others. Twelve hours later, Johnson dispatched forty-nine navy fighter-bombers to bomb a Vietcong training base at Dong Hoi, North Vietnam. Three days after that, there was another tit for tat: When the Vietcong blew up a hotel that housed American troops at Quinhon, killing twenty-three and injuring twenty-one, American planes responded with a three-hour attack against military depots in North Vietnam.

Secretary of Defense McNamara was not pleased with the results of these two reprisal attacks. Of the 491 buildings bombed, only forty-seven—fewer than 10 percent—had been destroyed, and only twenty-two had been damaged. The North Vietnamese could not meet American military might head-on, but they had antiaircraft weapons, some Soviet MIGs, and, above all, a great deal of ingenuity. The unfolding war was not as one-sided an affair as President Johnson had expected.

On March 2, Johnson authorized the long-planned Operation Rolling Thunder. A hundred American-piloted jets crossed the seventeenth parallel and attacked rail lines, supply facilities, an ammunition depot, and a naval base. Johnson, appearing on network television, told the American people, "I regret the necessities of war have compelled us to bomb North Vietnam. We have carefully limited those raids. They have been directed at concrete and steel and not at human life." This was not quite accurate: In 1965 U.S. planes conducted fifty-five thousand individual attacks over North Vietnam, dropping thirty-three thousand tons of TNT and, according to the CIA, killing thirteen thousand people, 80 percent of them civilians.

Another order issued by Johnson on March 2 also questioned his concern for human life: He authorized the use of napalm, an incendiary substance made of jellied gasoline. When napalm hits a human target, it sticks, burns for a long time, and almost literally melts the flesh. Napalm came to symbolize the American war in Vietnam, with its use of high-tech weaponry against people who were often defenseless noncombatants.

Still another order issued by Johnson on March 2 dispatched two U.S. Marine Corps units to Danang, bringing the total of American forces in South Vietnam to twenty-seven thousand.

Operation Rolling Thunder was a failure. It "seemed to stiffen rather than soften Hanoi's backbone," the Pentagon Papers later reported. The idea that destroying, or threatening to destroy, North Vietnam's industry would pressure Hanoi into calling it quits seems, in retrospect, to have been a colossal mistake. There really wasn't much to destroy. North Vietnam's gross national product was low even by Asian standards—less than two billion dollars a year. The Joint Chiefs of Staff found "only eight industrial installations" worth targeting.

Moreover, the Vietnamese were remarkably adept at coping with the American onslaught. Ho Chi Minh's people had been at war for twenty years—time enough to learn a few tricks. For instance, American pilots frequently tried to destroy the Ham Rong Bridge, seventy miles from Hanoi, which

Nguyen Van Thieu, President of South Vietnam, welcomes President
Lyndon Johnson to Vietnam in 1966. U.S. ARMY

Two U.S. Marines man
M-60 machine guns near the
Demilitarized Zone.

Napalm bombs explode on Vietcong structures south of Saigon.

A wounded U.S. soldier is transported to safety.

Thunderchief aircraft drop bombs on military transport bases used by the North Vietnamese.

Entrenched in a bunker, members of the 173rd Airborne Brigade wait out a lull in the fighting. UPI/BETTMANN

A soldier attempts to make radio contact during the Tet offensive.
U.S. ARMY

President Richard Nixon and Nguyen Van Thieu stroll on the grounds
of the Western White House in San Clemente, California. WHITE HOUSE

Soldiers on a search and destroy
mission make their way through
Vietnam's swampy jungle.
U.S. ARMY

A soldier comforts his wounded
comrade. UPI/BETTMANN

carried rail and road freight across the Song Ma River. On April 3, 1965, an attack force of seventy-nine planes assaulted the bridge with two-hundred-and-fifty-pound guided missiles and seven-hundred-and-fifty-pound bombs. But the planes did not destroy a single antiaircraft gun. Thirty-two missiles and a hundred and twenty-five bombs failed to do more than minor damage. The bridge remained intact, but two U.S. planes were shot down. Ham Rong was attacked over and over, and sometimes the bridge was put partially out of commission, but the Communists kept moving freight across the Song Ma on a pontoon bridge (a floating temporary bridge) partially submerged in the water to avoid detection.

American air attacks did destroy many bridges in the course of the war, but the Vietnamese either quickly repaired them or replaced them with pontoons. The North Vietnamese were clever, too, in dispersing their resources. They built underground factories and shelters and placed their petroleum in fifty-gallon drums all around the big cities, instead of in central storage areas. Despite the havoc wrought by the bombs, North Vietnam's gross national product actually increased during the bombing, in large part because of aid from the Soviet Union and China.

By the end of the war, the United States had dropped seven million tons of bombs on North Vietnam and South Vietnam, more than three times the bomb tonnage it had dropped on Europe and Asia in World War II. It had lost 918 planes and 818 flight-crew members. But the air war did not bring either North Vietnam or the Vietcong (officially the People's Revolutionary Army) to their knees; on the contrary, it seemed to boost the Communists' morale and determination to resist. During the beginning of Operation Rolling Thunder, North Vietnamese Premier Pham Van Dong refused an audience to a Canadian emissary who was supposed to assure the premier that the United States "has no designs on the territory of North Vietnam." And on March 29, the Vietcong blew up the American embassy in Saigon.

As the air war continued, President Johnson and the National Liberation Front (Vietcong) vied for world and domestic support. On March 22, 1965, the NLF issued a five-point statement accusing the United States of sabotaging the 1954 Geneva accords that were supposed to end the fighting and lead to a unified Vietnam. Speaking "on behalf of the fourteen million South Vietnamese people," the NLF pledged to "drive out the U.S. imperialists, liberate South Vietnam, and defend the North, with a view to the reunification of their fatherland."

Two weeks later, President Johnson made a speech defining the American goal—"to help South Vietnam defend its independence." That was a theme Johnson repeated over and over, stressing that South Vietnam must be an independent, separate *country*, not part of a *united* Vietnam that included both zones. The president also offered North Vietnam economic inducements to stop the fighting, such as an expensive plan, financed by the United States, to develop the Mekong Delta area.

On April 8, Premier Pham Van Dong issued a four-point statement demanding "recognition of the basic national rights of the Vietnamese people," including the right of those living in the South to settle their own "internal affairs . . . without any foreign interference." He called for "peaceful reunification" of North Vietnam and South Vietnam "without any foreign interference."

Johnson trod warily, trying, as he often said, "to preserve my options." "Hawks"—those who wanted a tougher military policy—criticized him for not going all out in the bombing; some even wanted him to use nuclear weapons. Late in 1967, when American forces were besieged by forty thousand Communist troops at Khe Sanh, a town near the Laotian border, Johnson and General William Westmoreland, then the American commander in Vietnam, actually did consider the use of nuclear weapons. But it was a passing notion, never put into practice.

As Johnson told one of his biographers, Doris Kearns, he always had to be careful to take no steps that might bring China or the Soviet Union into the war. He was willing to fight a limited war in Southeast Asia, even one in which thousands would die, but he was unwilling to contemplate the possibility of fighting a total war against the two powerful Communist powers. Such a war might easily lead to a nuclear confrontation, resulting in millions of deaths.

Because the bombing strategy failed, Johnson turned to the second alternative his staff had discussed in 1964—ground warfare. The bombing of North Vietnam was sustained and even intensified for the next three years, but the main focus now was on fighting the Vietcong in South Vietnam. In April and May 1965, this second phase of the war began. The Pentagon estimated at the time that the Vietcong "held sway over more than half of South Vietnam and could see the Saigon government crumbling before their very eyes." To cope with this state of affairs, the Johnson administration allowed General Westmoreland to increase his forces to eighty-two thousand and to devise a "victory strategy" using novel tactics and a variety of new weapons.

The United States had been helping the South Vietnamese and Laotian governments fight guerrillas since 1958, and had been sending advisers and contributing money to these governments for several years before that. The way to defeat a guerrilla force, American theorists believed, was to beat it at its own game. One senior U.S. official put it this way: "The Vietcong require a base of population to recruit or impress from, to transport ammunition and supplies, to grow goods, to supply information, to circulate propaganda, to hide among." The guerrilla had, in Mao Tse-tung's famous formulation, the same relationship to the community around him that a fish has to the ocean. So if you wanted to kill the fish all you would have to do is "dry up the ocean" by denying the guerrilla access to the people. This was called pacification.

Pacification, however, had been tried in Vietnam without much success. Local police and government officials had arbitrarily divided the rural population into two groups—"loyal" and "disloyal." These groups were then separated, taken from their homes, rice fields, and ancestral tombs, and relocated to "strategic hamlets." The typical strategic hamlet housed about a hundred families divided into groups of five, each group reporting on the "loyalty" of its members. Theoretically this arrangement would make it impossible for peasants to cooperate with the Vietcong.

But it didn't work that way. The number of "loyal" members in the rural areas was small—and they were intimidated and sometimes killed by sympathizers of the Vietcong. Moreover, the hamlet program was often carried out brutally, creating new enemies, rather than friends, for the South Vietnamese government and the United States. One reporter, Jonathan Schell, described a 1967 incident: U.S. soldiers surrounded the village of Ben Suc without warning, and other troops were dropped into the middle of the village. The entire population was rounded up, pushed into trucks, and transported to another place. During this chaotic episode, the village was burned, bulldozed, and bombarded by B-52s, so that no trace of it was left.

Under these circumstances, pacification was bound to be a monumental failure. Peasants resented having their old homes destroyed, doing forced labor to build the strategic hamlets or "new-life hamlets," and being increasingly dependent on American handouts to survive. They were not allowed to leave the hamlet from 6 P.M. to 8 A.M. Thus, as one South Vietnamese official lamented, "instead of separating the population from the Vietcong, we were making Vietcong."

General Westmoreland was confident that he could succeed where others had failed. He had a battery of special weapons particularly suited for fighting guerrillas and "drying up the ocean" where the fish swam. These weapons included thousands of low-flying helicopters, "cluster bombs" capable of dispersing hundreds of bomblets, an airplane called Puff the Magic Dragon that had three miniguns, each capable of shooting eighteen thousand rounds a minute, and chemical weapons dispensing CS, CN, and DM gas. The "Daisy-Cutter," a fifteen-thousand-pound bomb, could cut a hole three hundred feet in diameter, almost the size of a ball park, when dropped on a hilltop. Westmoreland also had use of the U.S. Army's Special Forces—the Green Berets—who tried to move around like guerrillas and were supposed to be adept at fighting "brushfire" wars. And he had the CIA to infiltrate the Vietcong.

At first, U.S. combat forces were assigned to coastal enclaves and instructed to go to the aid of South Vietnamese troops who were no more than fifty miles away. This, Washington believed, would put Americans at "relatively low risk." But in May and June 1965, the Vietcong won a number of major victories. On May 11, a Vietcong regiment attacked Songbe, capital of Phuoc Long province, and held the town for one day before withdrawing. Later in the month, the Vietcong ambushed a battalion of South Vietnamese troops near a town called Ba Gia. The battle lasted for a few days and ended in total defeat for the South Vietnamese army. The string of defeats continued into the next month and the month after.

Westmoreland was compelled to give up on the "enclave" strategy and adopt a more aggressive program—"search and destroy." That strategy seemed to work better because the South Vietnamese and American forces had tremendous superiority in firepower and could easily destroy a hamlet or a group of hamlets from afar.

But the Communists soon developed effective countertactics. They waited until American troops who were searching the hamlets in search and destroy missions were within a few yards, then hammered away with rifles and automatic weapons. Often they fought for only a few minutes, then vanished and set booby traps or laid mines. The Vietcong had access to a system of tunnels that dated back to the war against the French in the 1950s. The tunnels had been enlarged since then, so the Vietcong could pick and choose when to fight and when to melt away, and they usually fought only when the odds were with them. Their aim was not to hold territory but to inflict casualties on the Americans.

Thus, Westmoreland's forces were usually successful in the first phase of their attacks, when they set out to "destroy," but they almost invariably failed in the second phase, when their task was to "clear and hold." Stanley Karnow, an historian of the war, has written: "Another reality that frustrated U.S. troops in Vietnam was the enemy's ability to return to villages that had supposedly been cleaned out." In Binh Dinh province, for instance, American troops conducted four major drives and "inflicted nearly eleven thousand casualties on the North Vietnamese and Vietcong. But apart from its principal towns the province remained in Communist hands."

The first major battle between U.S. troops and the Vietcong took place in August 1965 on the Batangan Peninsula, where a regiment of the enemy was quietly massing near a new U.S. Marine Corps base at a place called Chu Lai. Two American battalions squeezed the Vietcong between them while fighter-bombers attacked guerrilla tunnels with napalm and a Navy cruiser lobbed shells from six-inch guns. After three days, the U.S. command admitted that forty-five marines had been killed in action and put the enemy's body count at 688.

On October 19, a North Vietnamese force of twenty-two hundred put a South Vietnamese camp under siege in the Central Highlands. The U.S. First Air Cavalry, sent in by helicopter and plane, came to the rescue. According to the army, only seven hundred of the twenty-two hundred enemy troops survived. Whether or not this was an accurate count, the action did not seem to devastate the North Vietnamese; in just a few weeks, they managed to deploy two thousand regulars near the Ia Drang River, where they were poised to overrun a Special Forces camp. On November 14, American helicopters put down four hundred and fifty men and officers in what seemed to be a pleasant clearing. It turned out to be a trap; the North Vietnamese were waiting in elephant grass eight feet high. The engagement at Ia Drang lasted about a month, and for the first time in Vietnam it involved B-52 bombers. The fighting, said General Westmoreland, was "as fierce as ever experienced by American troops." He claimed "1,771 known enemy casualties," as against 300 Americans killed.

These were large engagements—and there would later be some in which as many as twenty thousand U.S. troops saw action. But most confrontations were small affairs involving only a few hundred men fighting on unfavorable terrain, such as mountains and swamps, against an all-but-invisible enemy. Sometimes U.S. troops would encircle a village at night or early in the morning and then proceed to search every home for weapons, radio transmitters, and Vietcong. This was called "seal and search." Like "search and destroy," it inflicted much damage on the people in Vietnam's 12,500 hamlets but did not divorce the Vietcong from their supporters.

William Ehrhart, a former Marine Corps sergeant, explained to historian Stanley Karnow what happened in some of these forays: "We would go through a village before dawn, rousting everybody out of bed, and kicking down doors and dragging them out if they didn't move fast enough. They all had underground bunkers inside their huts to protect themselves against bombing and shelling. But to us the bunkers were Vietcong hiding places, and we'd blow them up with dynamite—and blow up the huts, too." The peasants were then "herded like cattle into a barbed wire compound, and left to sit there in the hot sun for the rest of the day, with no shade." Some would be taken away for interrogation by South Vietnamese police, who might beat and torture them. "If they weren't pro-Vietcong before we got there," Ehrhart says, "they sure as hell were by the time we left."

Westmoreland later claimed that, except in a few instances, "no American unit ... ever incurred what could fairly be called a setback" in the seven years that American forces were engaged in battle. Even if that were true, however, it didn't really matter. Once the U.S. troops moved out of an area—as they did in most instances—the Vietcong were again in control of the hamlets.

Americans might "capture" a Vietcong village, but they were usually unable to pacify it. The South Vietnamese government forces, which then took charge, were inept and unpopular. They represented a regime that was a cesspool of corruption, as even friendly observers admitted. The government was run by the military, and the generals who ruled each of the four areas into which the country was divided were primarily concerned with making their own fortunes by selling lower-ranking jobs to their subordinates. Not only the generals but every level of officer subsisted on graft. Many were in the game only to enrich themselves—by selling jobs, military equipment (sometimes to the Vietcong), and drugs, and by engaging in other illegal activities. With few exceptions they had little of the patriotic motivation that fired the Vietcong. The South Vietnamese rate of desertions was astronomical—ninety-six thousand in 1965 alone, or about one soldier in seven.

In a secret memorandum to President Johnson late in 1966, Secretary of Defense McNamara summarized the situation this way:

> Pacification has if anything gone backward. As compared with two, or four, years ago, enemy full-time regional forces and part-time guerrilla forces are larger; attacks, terrorism, and sabotage have increased in scope and intensity; more railroads are closed and highways cut; the rice crop ... is smaller; we control little, if any, more of the population. ...
> In essence, we find ourselves no better, and if anything, worse off.

5 THE WAR AT HOME

Every American war, going back to the Revolutionary War of 1776, has had some opposition among the civilian population. Sometimes the dissent was negligible, as in the Korean "police action" or World War II, sometimes it was active and vocal, as in the Mexican War of 1846. But opposition to the Vietnam War was so strong and sustained that it took on an unprecedented dimension, becoming known as The War at Home.

Small signs of that home-front war were already visible in 1963. On Easter Sunday in London, England, before a crowd of seventy thousand attending a Ban-the-Bomb rally, the world-renowned philosopher Bertrand Russell accused the United States of using "napalm jelly gasoline" and "chemical warfare" against the Vietnamese people. He called the U.S. effort a "war of annihilation."

An ocean away, at the United Nations Plaza in New York, a similar Ban-the-Bomb demonstration was under way before a much smaller crowd of six thousand. Again, however, two speakers raised the issue of U.S. military intervention in Vietnam. One was the seventy-eight-year-old Reverend A. J. Muste, a lifelong pacifist and radical. The other was Dave Dellinger, a Phi Beta Kappa from Yale University, also a pacifist, who had been sentenced to two years in prison during World War II for refusing to serve in the armed forces. Muste, Dellinger, and three others were editors of a small monthly magazine founded in 1956, *Liberation*, a publication dedicated to the nonviolent philosophy of Mahatma Gandhi of India. Many of *Liberation*'s editors and associate editors later played major roles in the Vietnam protest movement—Muste, Dellinger, Staughton Lynd, Tom Hayden, Dave McReynolds, and Sidney Lens, among others.

A number of small antiwar protests took place later that year while Mme. Ngo Dinh Nhu was on a speaking tour of American college campuses. Mme. Nhu, the wife of South Vietnam's secret-police chief and sister-in-law of Ngo Dinh Diem, infuriated students by sneering at the Buddhist monks who had burned themselves to death in protest against the Diem dictatorship. A strikingly beautiful woman—dubbed The Dragon Lady by American journalists—Mme. Nhu referred scornfully to "those miserable unarmed bonzes" (Buddhist monks) and announced, "I would clap hands at seeing another monk barbecue show." She was roundly booed and picketed by hundreds in San Francisco and at Columbia University, Harvard Law School, and the University of Michigan. "Down with the Nhu Frontier," read a placard carried by a picket in Detroit.

Concern over the deepening U.S. involvement in Indochina continued to intensify in 1964, spurred not only by the presidential election but also by a growing sense that the war was not going well. In Laos, a nation of only three million, American planes were conducting 12,500 sorties a month to make it difficult for the Vietnamese Communists to use the Ho Chi Minh Trail, which links North Vietnam and South Vietnam. A quarter of the population was driven from their homes or relocated. In May, opposition to the Vietnam War escalated when a recently organized radical youth group, the May 2 Movement (M-2-M), held demonstrations in San Francisco, New York, and other cities. M-2-M urged draft-age men to pledge that they would not fight in Vietnam. The pledge read: "We the undersigned are young Americans of draft age. We understand our obligation to defend our coun-

---

try and to serve in the armed forces but we object to being asked to support the war in Vietnam. . . . That war is for the suppression of the Vietnamese struggle for national independence.'' Toward the end of May, 149 young men announced in an advertisement in the *New York Herald Tribune* that they would not fight in Vietnam under any circumstances. A few days later, at Lafayette Square in Washington, D.C., demonstrators approved a Declaration of Conscience urging young people to ''resist the draft.''

This was a prelude to the massive demonstrations and civil disobedience that would soon follow. It was, in a sense, the culmination of protests against other conditions that had been ongoing for a decade—racial discrimination, nuclear testing and the nuclear arms race, and McCarthyism—a movement led by Senator Joseph R. McCarthy, who carelessly labeled people communists, causing them to lose their jobs and making many Americans afraid to dissent. It also reflected a major shift in the attitudes of young people—a cultural revolution away from the values of their parents toward a greater commitment to open inquiry, the questioning of authority, and the exploration of new forms in art, literature, music, and politics.

In December 1955, after Rosa Parks, a black woman, had been arrested in Montgomery, Alabama, for refusing to obey the law and give up her seat in the middle of a city bus to a white man, seventeen thousand black residents had begun a boycott of the bus system. They sparked a great civil rights movement that thrust into the limelight a twenty-six-year-old Baptist minister, the Reverend Martin Luther King, Jr. On another front, a movement developed against the House Committee on Un-American Activities, Senator Joseph R. McCarthy, and other right-wing forces seeking to curb dissent. A free-speech movement was born on the University of California's Berkeley campus, and some Americans joined with the Fair Play for Cuba Committee to show their support for Fidel Castro and the Cuban revolution. At harvest time, hundreds of young Americans went to Cuba to cut sugar-cane.

Other developments helped set the scene for the resistance to the Vietnam War. In 1957, Dr. Linus Pauling, a scientist who received the Nobel prize for chemistry in 1954 and the 1962 Nobel Peace Prize, circulated a petition to end nuclear testing because it would inflict cancer and death on hundreds of thousands of human beings. Nine thousand scientists around the world signed the petition. Moved by the same fears, an illustrator of children's books, Dagmar Wilson, called on women to conduct a "strike" on November 1, 1961, and was joined by thousands of women around the country, who refused to work that day in their homes and offices. Their anti-nuclear-testing movement, Women Strike for Peace, would eventually focus on the Vietnam War. And all of the traditional peace organizations—the American Friends Service Committee, the Fellowship of Reconciliation, the Women's International League for Peace and Freedom— which had been concentrating on nuclear disarmament, began turning their attention to Vietnam.

Perhaps the most significant development of the 1950s and 1960s was a profound change in human values and sensibilities. In the mid-1950s, some young people suddenly began expressing revulsion against conformity. A generation of writers—novelist Jack Kerouac, poet Alan Ginsberg, editor Paul Krassner, and others—lashed out against materialistic values, racial bigotry and discrimination, hypocrisy and government-sponsored propaganda, the arms race and the folly of building fallout shelters, the blacklisting of Americans for their political views, and the smugness of the older generation. A new kind of music called rock and roll swept the record charts, and a new counterculture with its own style and language took hold. "Beats" and their younger imitators, "hippies," began living in their own communities, such as the Haight-Ashbury district in San Francisco.

Unconcerned about careers, indifferent to saving money "for a rainy day," they lived for the moment. They smoked marijuana and later used LSD and other mind-altering drugs. They invented a new vocabulary—*man, beat, cool, hip, flip*—and were casual or uninhibited about sex, letting their hair grow long and casting aside three-piece suits and traditional dresses in favor of jeans, denim jackets, work boots, and army fatigues. Often referred to as "rebels without a cause," they adopted as their unofficial slogan the advice of Timothy Leary, a Harvard lecturer-turned-drug guru: "Turn on, tune in, drop out." As with the overwhelming majority of those who would soon be challenging the Vietnam War, they didn't engage in much sophisticated political analysis and refused to join the parties of the Old Left; they disliked what was going on in Communist Russia just as much as they disliked the way of life in Capitalist America.

Along with these "rebels without a cause," there also emerged in the 1960s some new groups of rebels who *did* have a cause—to create a better America, free of war and poverty. Sociologist C. Wright Mills called them the New Left.

In 1965 the best known and most active of these New Left organizations conceived the first major demonstration against the Vietnam War. Students for a Democratic Society (SDS) was not, from the start, an antiwar or anti-Vietnam organization. Its philosophy was set out in the Port Huron Statement, a declaration written by Tom Hayden in 1962:

We are the people of this generation, bred in at least modest comfort, housed now in universities, looking uncomfortably at the world we inherit. When we were kids the United States was the wealthiest and strongest country in the world . . . an initiator of the United Nations that we thought would distribute Western influence throughout the world. . . . As we grew, however, our comfort was penetrated by events too troubling to dismiss. The declaration "all men are created equal" . . . rang hollow before the facts of Negro life. . . . The proclaimed peaceful intentions of the United States contradicted its economic and military investments in the Cold War status quo. . . . We began to sense what we had originally seen as the American Golden Age was actually the decline of an era.

With the help of a $10,000 grant from the United Auto Workers, the SDS went to work in the civil rights movement and organized poor people in ten ghetto projects. Vietnam was by no means the organization's top priority until a well-known journalist, I. F. Stone, delivered a talk on the war to an SDS council meeting in December 1964. The members responded with a call for a march and rally in April 1965. "What kind of America is it," the call read, "whose response to poverty and oppression in Vietnam is napalm and defoliation? Whose response to poverty and oppression in Mississippi is—silence? It is a hideously *immoral* war. America is committing pointless murder."

By the time the march and rally took place on April 17, controversy over the U.S. role in Vietnam had moved to stage center. The American bombing of North Vietnam was making headlines, and people were reacting. In hundreds of communities, citizens with experience in the civil rights movement, the Fair Play for Cuba Committee, free-speech efforts, SDS chapters, or traditional peace groups, began organizing small demonstrations or vigils. A majority of Americans certainly still supported President Johnson, but the intensity of opposition to America's course in Southeast Asia was startling. Hundreds of thousands of people who had never been involved in political activities before were suddenly speaking out.

In March, forty-nine faculty members at the University of Michigan in Ann Arbor invented a new institution—the teach-in. Three thousand students and professors assembled and listened through the night to speakers on both sides of the issue. The atmosphere was informal—people came, went, left for private discussions, returned.

Meanwhile, preparations were under way for the April 17

march and rally. SDS did not feel it was strong enough to carry out the project by itself, so it solicited support from other student groups and adult peace organizations. A wide spectrum responded, including the American Friends Service Committee and the Committee for a Sane Nuclear Policy (SANE), then the largest peace organization in the country.

The coalition was strained from the outset by disputes over two issues. What should be done about Communist and Marxist groups that wanted to participate? SANE's policy was to exclude them because Communist participation would offend many Americans. But most of the other groups, led by SDS, insisted on a policy of nonexclusion, meaning that any group that wanted to participate was welcome, as long as it agreed with the objectives of the rally. A Communist who opposed the war had as much right to plan or march in an antiwar demonstration as a Democrat or Republican who opposed the war.

The other disagreement was on the issue of how the United States should extricate itself from Vietnam—"negotiate" or "withdraw." Moderates—again including SANE—called on President Johnson to negotiate with America's adversary in Vietnam. The rest of the coalition argued that there was nothing to negotiate about—the United States had no business being in Vietnam in the first place, and its only "right" was to get out immediately. "Nonexclusion" and "immediate withdrawal" became central themes of the antiwar movement for the next seven years; such moderate elements as SANE, which rejected those principles, steadily lost influence.

The April 17 rally drew twenty thousand protesters to Washington. The turnout was considered large at the time— the organizers had expected only about half that number— but was small compared to the marches of half a million and three-quarters of a million that would come later. The demonstrators marched down Pennsylvania Avenue, picketed the White House, then held a rally near the Washington

Monument. Staughton Lynd, a lifelong pacifist and a major figure in the 1964 civil rights summer campaign, presided. Speakers included Senator Ernest Gruening, of Alaska, who had voted against the Tonkin Gulf Resolution; journalist I. F. Stone; Robert Moses, a civil rights leader who had been active in registering black voters in the South; and the twenty-two-year-old president of SDS, Paul Potter. The mood of the young crowd was expressed in the folk songs of Judy Collins, Joan Baez, and the Freedom Voices. The participants shouted approval for a petition to Congress to "end, not extend, the war in Vietnam."

One feature that would characterize the anti-Vietnam protest movement was already evident—its decentralized nature. There was no formal leadership. Someone would get an idea and put it into practice; if it was a good idea, it caught on.

The teach-in, for instance, spread swiftly to scores of campuses. Typically, a group calling itself the Universities Committee on the Problems of War and Peace of Greater New York joined with the Pratt Institute chapter of the National Student Association to hold a teach-in for the students and faculty members of four Brooklyn colleges. Ten speakers, most of them assistant professors, addressed the group for twenty minutes each, then took questions for ten minutes. Among the speakers was at least one "hawk," who pleaded for ultimate victory in Vietnam.

The teach-in tactic was used throughout the war, but it reached a peak of sorts almost immediately. On May 15, 1965, 100,000 people at 122 schools were linked by a national radio hookup to hear prominent speakers either defend or attack the Johnson policy. Speaking in favor of what the government was doing were historian Arthur Schlesinger, Jr.; Zbygniew Brzezinski, of Columbia University; Wesley R. Fishel, of Michigan State; and Robert A. Scalapino, of the University of California at Berkeley. The prize draw of the debate, presidential assistant McGeorge Bundy, cancelled at the last moment. Speaking in opposition to the government's policy were equally prominent figures, such as Hans J. Morgenthau, of the University of Chicago; Stanley Millet, of Briarcliff College; Mary Wright, of Yale; author Issac Deutscher; and George McTurnan Kahin, of Cornell.

Toward the end of the same month, crowds ranging from ten thousand to thirty thousand attended the Vietnam Day teach-in at Berkeley, where they listened to the famous pediatrician, Dr. Benjamin Spock; author Norman Mailer; comedian Dick Gregory; socialist Norman Thomas; and Senator Gruening. Speakers favoring the government position failed to show up.

The resistance to the war gained momentum after April 1965. Everyone, it seemed, had ideas about how to end the war. The Center for the Study of Democratic Institutions, headed by a world-famous educator, Robert M. Hutchins, gave a grant to a young writer, Robert Scheer (who later joined the *Los Angeles Times*), to write a pamphlet on "How the United States Got Involved in Vietnam." At a time when few knew the origins of the war, Scheer's analysis had tremendous impact.

In June, the Reverend A. J. Muste organized a Speak-Out at the Pentagon, an early act of civil disobedience against the war; many others would follow. Gandhian doctrine held that it was permissible to violate an immoral law or one that protected immoral acts. Martin Luther King, Jr., and his followers had invoked that principle when they violated southern laws forbidding blacks to drink at "white" water fountains or to use "white only" rest rooms. In the same spirit, Henry David Thoreau had refused to pay taxes during the Mexican War in 1847—and had gone to jail for his act of civil disobedience.

Muste and some two hundred fellow demonstrators were following in that tradition and intended to subject themselves to arrest. They began the Speak-Out at the Pentagon by distributing thirty thousand leaflets to the military personnel and civilian employees at the massive Defense Department headquarters. Then the protesters entered the building and held public meetings. In accordance with Gandhian principles, they carefully avoided committing any act of violence.

During the Speak-Out, six of the protest organizers held a thirty-minute meeting with Defense Secretary McNamara. They pointed out that the Pentagon itself had concluded in one of its studies that it would take at least ten and perhaps as many as fifteen regular troops to contain just one guerrilla. "Since you say that there are two hundred and forty thousand Vietcong," the group told McNamara, "that would mean you need two-and-a-half to three million troops to hold them in check. Apart from the fact that the war is immoral, where will you get the three million soldiers to win it?" McNamara gave the kind of answer often heard from government officials: "I can't discuss that with you. We know things that you don't."

When the demonstration had lasted a couple of hours, the authorities found a way to end the protest without making any arrests: Hundreds of police and security officers formed a phalanx around the group and pushed it, step by step, out of the building. The Speak-Out at the Pentagon did not get the kind of public attention Muste had hoped for, but it was the first step in establishing a national antiwar leadership.

The next step occurred a few weeks later when a group calling itself the Assembly of Unrepresented People convened to hold a number of workshops in Washington and then started marching toward the Capitol. More than three hundred were arrested as police stopped the marchers on Capitol Hill. Members of a right-wing group tossed red paint at Dave Dellinger and Staughton Lynd as they walked arm in arm, and a photograph of this incident appeared on the cover of *Life*—one of the largest mass-circulation magazines at the time—and in hundreds of newspapers.

By now, the bombing of North Vietnam had been supplemented by the dispatch of American ground troops. Antiwar forces responded by redoubling their efforts. At Berkeley, the Vietnam Day Committee issued a call for the first International Days of Protest, to be held in the United States and abroad on October fifteenth and sixteenth. The first day was to be a typical community protest meeting, but it was to be followed on October sixteenth by "massive civil disobedience."

Preparations for the International Days of Protest led to the formation of the first national antiwar group—the National Coordinating Committee to End the War in Vietnam (NCC), with headquarters in Madison, Wisconsin. The NCC was neither particularly effective nor prominently visible, but its call for protest actions on October fifteenth and sixteenth was heeded in ninety-three cities and drew more than a hundred thousand participants. A thousand people rallied in Chicago; thirteen thousand in New York; fifteen thousand in Berkeley on the first day and five thousand on the second.

In New York, as the demonstrators paraded down Fifth Avenue hecklers pelted them with paint, eggs, and tomatoes. As the Berkeley demonstrators marched through Oakland they were intercepted by four hundred city police and a hundred counterdemonstrators, and it seemed for a time that there might be a bloody confrontation. On the second day, the marchers were harassed by members of the Hell's Angels motorcycle gang, who shouted, "America for the Americans."

At the State Department, the official spokesman, Robert McCloskey, dismissed the protest actions as representing only "an infinitesimal fraction of the American people." The "vast majority," he said, supported President Johnson's policies in Vietnam. *New York Times* columnist James Reston wrote that the demonstrators were "not promoting peace but postponing it." General Maxwell Taylor, former ambassador to Vietnam, agreed that the demonstrators would "prolong the war."

One consequence of the October 1965 events was the

formation of city-wide coalitions. In New York, Norma Becker, a schoolteacher and leader of the War Resisters League, formed the Fifth Avenue Peace Parade Committee, together with Dave Dellinger and Reverend A. J. Muste. It included a hundred and fifty groups. In Chicago, Sidney Lens and business publisher Henry Wineberg formed the Chicago Peace Council, which had thirty affiliates. Similar coalitions emerged in the San Francisco Bay Area, Cleveland, and most other major cities.

Other innovative antiwar tactics included efforts to establish contact with the "enemy" so that Americans would begin to think of the people in the NLF and North Vietnam as ordinary human beings seeking nothing more than to till their land and raise their families. Ten members of Women Strike for Peace met with ten Vietnamese women in Jakarta, Indonesia. The Vietnamese showed the Americans pictures of bombed homes and hospitals, devastated villages, and dead civilians; they talked for five days about their husbands, children, shopping, and other daily events. Back home, the American women issued a widely circulated statement calling for U.S. withdrawal. "As women," it said, "we cannot rest until Vietnamese children, American children, all children, are free to grow up in peace and security."

The next meeting with Vietnamese was even more dramatic—and controversial. Herbert Aptheker, an American Marxist scholar, arranged a trip to *North* Vietnam for Staughton Lynd, then a history professor at Yale, and Tom Hayden of SDS. In time, many people would make this trek—most of them, like Lynd and Hayden, non-Communists—but in 1965, the outcry around the country was deafening: This was "treason," visiting the "enemy" during wartime. Yale alumni demanded that Lynd be fired.

A few months after the Lynd-Hayden-Aptheker visit to North Vietnam, Muste took a delegation of six pacifists to Saigon, South Vietnam, to hold a demonstration on the scene. Their press conference was disrupted by police, their lives threatened, their leaflets confiscated, and they were quickly deported. But they had made their point—South Vietnam was hardly the democratic country the Johnson administration claimed it was.

Another form of protest initiated in 1965 and greatly expanded over the next few years was resistance to the draft. The law provided that young men between the ages of eighteen-and-a-half and twenty-six had to register for induction into military service. Each month, about thirty thousand were drafted. At first, college students were deferred, but a change in the rules early in 1966 put students with lower grades into the eligible class.

Opposition to the draft had started even before American troops were sent to Vietnam; now it took on a new form— draft-card burning. During the October International Days of Protest, David J. Miller, of the *Catholic Worker*, a newspaper concerned with social action, burned his draft card in front of an induction center in New York City. The event was captured by television cameras and broadcast nationally. Miller's act was especially dramatic because Congress had passed a law in August making such an action a felony punishable by up to five years in prison. Miller was arrested and eventually served a two-year term. Two weeks after his protest, in front of the Federal Court House in Foley Square, two other pacifists burned their cards while two hundred supporters carried signs: "Burn Draft Cards, Not Children" and "Would Christ Carry a Draft Card?" Over the next few years, thousands of young men publicly burned their draft cards or turned them in to the authorities. Like Miller, many served prison terms.

On November 2, a thirty-two-year-old Quaker, Norman R. Morrison, went further: Following the example set by the Vietnamese Buddhist monks, he poured kerosene over himself near the Pentagon and set himself afire, leaving a family behind. Another Quaker, eighty-two-year-old Alice Herz, had burned herself to death in March in a similar protest action, and a few days after Morrison's death, Roger A. LaPorte, of the Catholic Worker movement, also immolated himself, this time in front of the United Nations.

Still, many voices were raised in defense of government policy, and sometimes peace demonstrators themselves became the targets of violent attacks. In Chicago, Women for Peace held a two-hour antiwar vigil every Saturday in the center of the city—a vigil they kept up, rain or shine, for eight years. It was not uncommon for passersby to spit at the women or seize their leaflets. Though the antiwar sentiment at Berkeley was extremely strong, there also were those who supported the war. Twenty-six professors publicly assailed the Vietnam Day Committee. FBI Director J. Edgar Hoover attacked the demonstrators as "halfway citizens who are neither morally, mentally, nor emotionally mature." In New York the City Council voted overwhelmingly to convert Veterans Day into a Support American Vietnam Effort Day.

Nonetheless, antiwar activity continued and increased. The last big national rally of 1965 was held in front of the Washington Monument in the nation's capital over the Thanksgiving weekend. It was sponsored by SANE—that organization's last major action during the war—and drew thirty-five thousand. Among the participants were fifteen hundred members of the National Coordinating Committee to End the War in Vietnam, who were holding a conference in Washington the same weekend, and many young people who belonged to such radical groups as M-2-M, Youth Against War and Fascism, the Socialist Workers Party, the Young Socialist Alliance, and the Du Bois Clubs.

The rally posed some problems for the moderate SANE. It didn't want leftists to participate, but short of using force, there was no way to stop them from marching. In an attempt to retain its respectable image of reasonableness, SANE produced a group of endorsers and speakers that included Coretta Scott King, the widow of Dr. Martin Luther King, Jr.;

playwright Arthur Miller; authors John Hersey and Saul Bellow; and the venerable socialist Norman Thomas.

SANE distributed small American flags to the marchers so that the affair would have a patriotic flavor. Participants were asked to confine their placards to seventeen approved slogans, and signs demanding "Immediate Withdrawal" or "Bring the GIs Home Now" were pointedly excluded. Still the young radicals and their radical placards could not be kept out. Here and there, in fact, demonstrators could be seen carrying the Vietcong flag, a yellow star on a blue panel, and the speaker who received the most applause was SDS president Carl Oglesby, who spoke in support of revolution.

"We are here," Oglesby said, "to protest against a growing war. Since it is a very bad war, we acquire the habit of thinking that it must be caused by very bad men." The men responsible for this evil war, however, were "all liberals"—Truman, Eisenhower, Kennedy, McGeorge Bundy, McNamara, Lyndon Johnson. Perhaps, Oglesby suggested, there are "two quite different liberalisms: One authentically humanist; the other not so human at all."

The war in Vietnam, he continued, "is also a revolution, as honest a revolution as you can find anywhere in history. And this is a fact which all our intricate official denials will never change. . . . But it doesn't make any difference to our leaders anyway. Their aim . . . is to safeguard what they take to be American interests around the world against revolution or revolutionary change, which they always call communism."

6 "JOIN US, JOIN US"

The war in Vietnam and the war at home grew fiercer at the end of 1965 and in 1966 and 1967.

The U.S. bombing of North Vietnam continued and expanded, coming ever closer to the North's two main cities, Hanoi and Haiphong. On December 15, 1965, American planes destroyed a power plant fourteen miles from Haiphong that supplied 15 percent of North Vietnam's electricity. It was a severe blow to Ho Chi Minh's government—particularly since the bombing occurred just six days after President Johnson had expressed a willingness to negotiate an end to the war.

"This act of the United States," said Hanoi radio, "is part of its peace hoax. It is known to everybody that each time the U.S. imperialists jabbered about peaceful negotiations they intensified and expanded the war in Vietnam." In June 1966, the air raids reached the very outskirts of Hanoi and Haiphong.

Just as important to the U.S. military plan as the air war against the North was the bombing of the Ho Chi Minh Trail, a heavily wooded series of paths that ran for six hundred miles parallel to South Vietnam's border with Laos and Cambodia. Down this route North Vietnam sent men—mostly on foot or bicycle, but sometimes by truck—and some supplies, on a journey that usually took six weeks. About thirty-six thousand North Vietnamese passed down the trail in 1965 to fight alongside the NLF in the South, and in 1966 the number approached ninety thousand.

U.S. planes dropped chemicals along the trail to defoliate the areas, which removed leaves from the trees that shielded the infiltrators. But despite the bombings and the hardships, such as malaria and amoebic dysentery, that took many lives along the way, the trail could not be put out of commission. General Westmoreland was willing to invade Laos with an attack force of three divisions to cut off the infiltration route, but President Johnson vetoed the idea in favor of erecting a billion-dollar "electronic fence"—an electrified barbed wire barrier surrounded by mine fields that would stretch sixty miles across. But when construction began in 1967, the North Vietnamese stymied the plan by placing the entire area under siege. The Johnson administration was forced to give up the idea, contenting itself with an increase in air strikes against the trail from three hundred a day to nine hundred.

Neither the defoliation nor the bombing, however, was able to stop Hanoi's infiltration of men and supplies.

On the ground in South Vietnam, General Westmoreland's forces continued to conduct hundreds of small search-and-destroy missions. But they also mounted attacks that involved thousands and even tens of thousands of troops—campaigns that lasted for weeks or months. Westmoreland was convinced he could achieve victory by the end of 1967 and stepped up the war to achieve that goal. Operation Masher, early in 1966, was an assault by twenty thousand American and allied troops from many countries against regular North Vietnamese forces stationed in the central province of Binh Dinh. Westmoreland claimed that an entire enemy division had been destroyed. Some villages in the area were designated "free-fire zones," that is, all their inhabitants were considered pro-Vietcong, so U.S. troops could shoot them without worrying about further inquiry or punishment.

When Operation Masher was over, American forces attacked the coastal region of Binh Dinh, dropping seven hundred and fifty tons of bombs from giant B-52 bombers and using two hundred and ninety-two thousand pounds of napalm. In the middle of 1966, two divisions were sent to the West Central Highlands to intercept a large North Vietnamese contingent, and the First Infantry Division conducted a campaign to open fifty miles of Route 13 between Saigon and Binh Long province. The road was partially cleared in June and July 1966, but by October one Vietcong division and one North Vietnamese regiment had returned to the area. In the ensuing Operation Attleboro, American GIs from three infantry divisions and twenty-two thousand South Vietnamese fought what was, up to that point, the largest battle of the war. It lasted into November.

In 1967, the first of the year's large campaigns, Operation Cedar Falls, mounted a full-scale attack on a Vietcong stronghold called the Iron Triangle, which was only twenty-five miles from Saigon. Some seven thousand villagers, as well as guerrillas, were driven from their homes, and the village was plowed under. Later, Operation Junction City was mounted in a region called War Zone C, beyond the Iron Triangle. American officers were convinced that this was the command center for the Vietcong—known as COSVN—and assigned thirty thousand U.S. troops and four Vietnamese battalions to find and destroy it. But no command center was found.

As was the case with Westmoreland's other major operations, he rated Operation Junction City a "success"— twenty-one villages were demolished, their people killed, wounded, or placed in "pacification" camps. Westmoreland's headquarters issued news releases proclaiming that the NLF was "through forever" in this war zone and that there was "no chance left for the foe." But months later, when the NLF launched its biggest campaign of the war, the Tet offensive, one of the major thrusts came from this very war zone.

Operation Junction City was the war's last large battle by concentrated U.S. forces. Another offensive in 1967, Operation Fairfax, involved thousands of GIs, but they were broken into hundreds of small units and sent to patrol the countryside around Saigon day and night.

Had all the American campaigns succeeded in bringing the war to an end, or even under control, the opposition at home would probably have faded. But in 1966 and 1967, victory in Vietnam seemed as elusive as ever, and in 1968 the prospects of terminating the war successfully became even dimmer. American troops might clear an area but they could not hold it. The South Vietnamese soldiers assigned to "pacify" the cleared villages were inept and lacked motivation. Even General Westmoreland was forced to comment that their "pace was rather slow. They did take off on weekends. They had extended holidays. They were far from diligent in pursuance of the war."

In 1966, more than one out of five South Vietnamese soldiers deserted the army. "The ARVN soldiers fought badly," observes foreign correspondent Frances Fitzgerald, "not so much because they were badly trained as because they had nothing to fight for."

All too often, villages that were called "cleared" had simply been destroyed, their inhabitants turned into refugees. Some four million villagers—a quarter of South Vietnam's population—were driven to the cities, where they faced an alien way of life that drew them into either poverty or corruption. Saigon and Cholon (a section of Saigon), which had a combined population of only a half million before America fully joined the war, grew to three million. Some prospered as a result of this uprooting; they learned the ways of criminals, prostitutes, and hustlers. The experience made most of them unfriendly to their own government as well as to the Americans.

The South Vietnamese central government continued to pose major problems. In the first months after the war was Americanized, Vietnamese regimes came and went, one general replacing another as the man in charge. In June 1965, after still another coup, Air Vice Marshall Nguyen Cao Ky took over as head of government and remained in power for two years, until the September 1967 elections, which placed General Nguyen Van Thieu in the presidency with Ky as vice president.

From the beginning to the end of the American war, the South Vietnamese military government was marked by un-bridled corruption. Because the officers and their cronies grew rich off American aid, much of which they stole and sold, the South Vietnamese foot soldiers often lacked ammu-nition and grenades. "The generals," said Frank Snepp, the CIA's chief strategy analyst in Saigon, "siphoned off the aid money we were directing to the government."

"Within weeks," after Ky came to power, observes histo-rian Michael Maclear, "vast quantities of U.S. materiel arrived—and much of it just as quickly vanished. . . . Saigon received forty garbage trucks; several were immediately stolen. Overnight, vehicle thefts became an industry."

"The corruption system in Vietnam," wrote Pulitzer Prize winner Peter Arnett of the Associated Press, "begins right at the very top. It begins in Saigon. And the officials milk each other right down to the lowest level. . . . The province level officials virtually buy their jobs. And the corps commander—the warlord—he is the one who gets the eventual payment." This was not an atmosphere that would promote idealism and self-sacrifice.

A Buddhist revolt in 1966 showed that there was little popular support for the South Vietnamese government. Early in March, Premier Ky announced that General Nguyen Chanh Thi, the commander of the First Corps—who was sympathetic to the Buddhists—had resigned because of a sinus ailment and intended to go to the United States for treatment. The next day, however, it became obvious that there was more to the matter than the condition of Thi's nasal passages. The United Buddhist Church issued a communiqué demanding that the military junta in Saigon hold elections for a civilian government. A day later, there were protest demonstrations in Hue, Danang, Hoi An, and other coastal cities in the First Corps area. Banners demanded the resignation of Ky and his two closest associates, General Nguyen Huu Co and General Nguyen Van Thieu.

During the following week, the demonstrations grew larger and spread to other cities, including Saigon. In Danang, thousands of government employees and soldiers marched with dock workers, chanting slogans against the government and against the Americans. The port of Danang had to be shut down. Students demonstrated against corruption, and anti-American slogans began to be heard everywhere. Placards in Hue read, "Down with the CIA, end the foreign domination of our country, end the oppression of the yellow race."

As the situation continued to deteriorate, the government declared Danang an "enemy-held city," even though the Vietcong had nothing to do with the Buddhist revolt. When Ky and Co tried to land at the Danang air base with fifteen hundred troops, they could get no farther than the runway and were forced to return to Saigon. Vietnamese marines were evacuated from the base by American transports.

During this hectic period, students and young workers burned down the American consulate and the United States Information Service library in Hue. At about this time, too, a Buddhist nun set her gasoline-soaked clothes afire and burned to death, leaving a note that criticized President Johnson for supporting the military junta. The next day, twenty thousand demonstrators came out in Saigon, and eight other bonzes and nuns burned themselves to death.

Ironically, the Buddhists were demanding exactly what the Johnson administration claimed to have in mind for South Vietnam—free elections and a civilian government—

but they didn't believe the Americans would help them win those objectives. Many, perhaps most, wanted the Americans to get out of their country altogether.

The Buddhist revolt ended after four months. Students and union leaders were jailed; when they eventually were released, many joined the NLF. The elections they had sought turned out to be much like the twelve previous ones: Four candidates who favored a cease-fire and peace were ruled off the ballot. Two generals—Ky and Thieu—made a deal, approved by the other top generals, in which Thieu accepted the presidential nomination and Ky the nomination for vice president.

Back home in the United States, the uncertain situation in Vietnam prompted many people to question why their government had become involved in the first place. As a rule, Americans give their government full support in wartime, but by the beginning of 1966 that support was clearly weakening—not only among the radical pacifists and students who were burning draft cards but also in Congress and other moderate and conservative circles.

To appease the critics, President Johnson ordered a pause in the bombing of North Vietnam from December 24, 1965, until January 31, 1966, and invited the North Vietnamese government in Hanoi to "negotiate." But no one expected much to come of this offer, since the United States demanded that North Vietnam recognize South Vietnam as an independent country and leave it alone, whereas North Vietnam demanded that the United States withdraw all "foreign" military forces, as provided in the 1954 Geneva accords.

While the bombing pause was under way Chairman J. William Fulbright, of the Senate Foreign Relations Committee, announced he had begun to have second thoughts about the war: He questioned whether the Tonkin Gulf Resolution gave Johnson all the war-making powers the president claimed. Late in January, Fulbright's committee held nationally televised hearings at which both the administration and its critics were heard. Only one critic, Senator Wayne Morse, of Oregon, argued for U.S. withdrawal from Vietnam, but others, including Fulbright, were now willing to admit that American intervention was a mistake.

A couple of days before the bombing pause was to end, twenty-nine senators called on Johnson to extend it. In mid-February, Senator Robert F. Kennedy, a brother of the slain President John F. Kennedy, proposed that Johnson should allow the NLF "a share of power" in South Vietnam to encourage it to make a "negotiated settlement." In April, Fulbright delivered a series of lectures in which he questioned America's "arrogance of power," and other prominent Americans began to express similar views. Among them was America's best-known syndicated columnist, Walter Lippmann, who predicted that the president would soon find himself on "a dead-end street" if he didn't change his policy. "The division of the country will simply grow as the casualties and costs increase," Lippmann wrote.

Wherever one turned in 1966 and 1967, some kind of antiwar action was taking place—four hundred Quakers picketing the White House, innumerable teach-ins, newspaper advertisements stating opposition to the war, lobbying by Women Strike for Peace, fasts at various colleges, vigils. Lyndon Johnson could travel to no destination in the country, except for military bases, without encountering antiwar pickets shouting, "Hey, hey, LBJ, how many kids did you kill today?"

Early in 1966, the president went to Honolulu for a strategy conference with Vietnamese and American officials. Antiwar demonstrators met him at the airport in Oahu, and again on his way home in Los Angeles. At a Waldorf-Astoria Hotel dinner in New York City, where Johnson received a National Freedom Award, four thousand opponents of the war picketed outside and listened to A. J. Muste denounce the war. Inside at the dinner, Jim Peck, a veteran of the civil rights freedom rides, rose as Johnson began speaking and shouted three times, "Mr. President, peace in Vietnam." He was hauled away by police and sentenced to sixty days in jail.

In late March, the Second International Days of Protest took place under the auspices of the National Coordinating Committee to End the War in Vietnam (NCC). Demonstrations were held in more than a hundred cities around the world. The New York group, which included several hundred veterans of previous wars, including Korea, was estimated at between twenty and fifty thousand.

There were a few jarring notes, confirming Walter Lippmann's warning about "divisions" in the country. Hecklers in New York, some wearing American Legion insignia, threw eggs at the antiwar marchers, and a few attacked young people carrying NLF flags. *The New York Daily News*, reflecting the severity of the division in the nation, commented, "The Saturday shenanigans gave aid and comfort to the enemy in time of war and thereby fitted the U.S. Constitution's definition of treason." In Chicago, where five thousand marched, SANE and the American Friends Service Committee withdrew from the event in protest when leaders of the march called for unconditional withdrawal of U.S. troops and its policy of "nonexclusion." Nevertheless, the crowd in Chicago was much larger than the one that had turned out the previous October, and in New York, the *Herald Tribune* noted that "the marchers this time seemed to represent much more of a cross section of Americans."

Many new groups were being formed to express opposition to the war. One was Clergy and Laymen Concerned About the War in Vietnam, which included such prominent clerics as Dr. John C. Bennett, president of the prestigious Union Theological Seminary; Rabbi Maurice Eisendrath, president of the Union of American Hebrew Congregations; and the Reverend William Sloane Coffin, Jr., chaplain of Yale University. In 1966, Clergy and Laymen received a grant of $1.5 million from a liberal foundation and established a network of staff and offices around the country. Under the Reverend Richard Fernandez, its executive director, Clergy and Laymen not only mobilized thousands of religious people for antiwar activities but also added a touch of respectability to the movement. It was difficult to denounce it as "Communist" when so many non-Communist clerics were involved in its work.

Another group that helped spark what became known as the Movement was the Resistance, a network of organizations whose members were determined not to go to war even if it meant jail or exile. Their most conspicuous activity was to burn their draft cards publicly or turn them back to the authorities; both actions were violations of the law and subjected the protesters to up to five years in prison and $10,000 in fines. On the initiative of a group at Cornell University, 175 young men stood on a rock in New York City's Central Park on April 15, 1967, and publicly burned their draft cards. That same day, at Kezar Stadium in San Francisco, the former president of the student body at Stanford University, David Harris, urged a national turn-in of draft cards on October 16. This form of protest persisted throughout the war, and it included not only draft-card burning but also refusal to register for the draft and refusal to serve in the military. One of those who refused to be inducted into the army was the heavyweight boxing champion of the world, Muhammad Ali. He cited religious grounds but was stripped of his title anyway—and convicted. After the war, he was vindicated by the courts.

Perhaps more dramatic were the invasions of draft board headquarters by a group of radical Catholics beginning in October 1967. That month a priest named Philip Berrigan and three friends broke into a Baltimore draft office, poured their own blood and some duck blood on draft records, then waited patiently for the FBI to arrive on the scene and arrest them.

Six months later, Philip Berrigan and his brother Daniel, a

Jesuit priest, along with seven other demonstrators, performed a similar invasion of a draft board in Catonsville, Maryland. They seized 378 files of young men about to be inducted, took the files across the road, and burned them with homemade napalm. Then they waited for the police to arrest them. While they sat in jail, dozens of others began to use the same technique elsewhere to dramatize their religious conviction that the Vietnam war was sacrilegious.

The antidraft movement was active even in the military services. In June 1966, three U.S. Army privates training at Fort Hood, Texas, decided they would refuse to serve in Indochina, as they were scheduled to the following month. With the support of Muste, Dellinger, Lynd, and others, they held a press conference and made their announcement. The privates were tried by court martial and ultimately served two years in prison. There would be others like them, however. Eventually, too, there would be a number of antiwar coffee shops near military installations, where young people in the armed forces could gather after duty hours, and a few dozen antiwar newspapers published within the armed forces by GIs.

The Movement seemed to find a way of involving itself in any opportunity that would help to raise the antiwar issue. In May 1966, some eight thousand demonstrators in Washington displayed seventy-three thousand "voter pledges" they had gathered from citizens who promised to vote only for candidates who favored a cease-fire and negotiations with the Vietcong. The next day, President Johnson publicly condemned the "Nervous Nellies . . . who turn on their own leaders, their own country, and their own fighting men."

But critics of the war found many ways to express their opposition. Hundreds, then thousands, refused to pay federal income taxes or excise taxes placed on all telephone bills by the government. At some colleges and universities, students seized administration offices for a few days in protest against

Martin Luther King, Jr., speaks out against the war during a panel discussion at Riverside Church in New York City (1967).

JOHN C. GOODWIN

Members of the Resistance hold a draft card turn-in.
JOHN C. GOODWIN

A New York City antiwar demonstration held in April 1967, attracts unprecedented numbers. JOHN C. GOODWIN

Peace activists relax on a rock in
New York's Central Park during
April 1967 demonstration.
JOHN C. GOODWIN

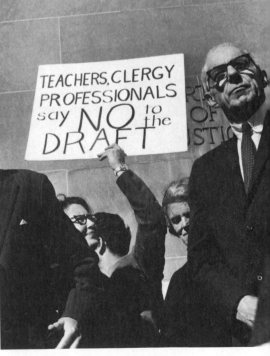

Dr. Benjamin Spock, the
Reverend William Sloane Coffin,
Jr., and others present 1,000
draft cards to the office of the
U.S. Attorney General.
JOHN C. GOODWIN

Sidney Lens addresses the crowd during an October 1967 rally in Washington, D.C.
JOHN C. GOODWIN

Protesters set up coffins, representing the war dead, in front of the Capitol.
JOHN C. GOODWIN

Protesters march from the Lincoln Memorial to the Pentagon.

JOHN C. GOODWIN

A demonstrator is arrested during a march on the Pentagon in 1967. JOHN C. GOODWIN

These two nuns are members of CALCAV—Clergy and Laymen Concerned About the War in Vietnam. JOHN C. GOODWIN

As the Chicago Eight trial begins in 1969, Jerry Rubin, David Dellinger, and Abbie Hoffman (from left to right) hold a press conference. AP/WIDE WORLD

Folk singers Peter Yarrow and Pete Seeger entertain a crowd of protesters in Washington, D.C. in November 1969. JOHN C. GOODWIN

Growing anti-Nixon sentiment is expressed by a peace activist at a rally for the impeachment of Nixon (1974). JOHN C. GOODWIN

their schools' collaboration with the government in the war effort. When the Selective Service system announced it would test the aptitude of high school seniors and college students to determine whether they were entitled to deferments from service, four hundred students seized the administration building of the University of Chicago for three days to protest the university's cooperation with the government. Students at City College in New York held a sit-in in the office of the college president. There were vigils, picket lines outside draft boards, marches, letters to the press and to members of Congress, sit-ins at Congressional offices, newspaper advertisements.

These various protests may have seemed chaotic, as if the antiwar movement had no direction, but throughout the war one or another central coalition always gave the Movement focus. When, once or twice a year, that coalition issued a call for a national demonstration, people from all over the country responded.

The first such coalition, the National Coordinating Committee to End the War in Vietnam (NCC), lasted only a few months. It was replaced by a more durable coalition, which changed its name each time it planned a major action but was popularly known as the Mobe. The initiative came from a group of professors who called themselves the Inter-University Committee for Debate on Foreign Policy. Most of the members had been active in the teach-ins of 1965 and were now turning their attention to the Congressional elections of 1966. They hoped, as their statement put it, "to promote the candidacy of opponents of the war."

That was also the goal of such moderate organizations as SANE, which fielded two dozen antiwar candidates for Congressional seats that year, though only one came close to winning an election—Robert Scheer, in the San Francisco Bay Area, who garnered 45 percent of the vote in a campaign against an incumbent member of Congress.

During the 1966 elections, in Dearborn, Michigan, home

of the big Ford auto plant, a referendum was held on the question: "Are you in favor of an immediate cease-fire and withdrawal of U.S. troops from Vietnam so that the Vietnamese people can settle their own affairs?" To the surprise of most observers, 40 percent (14,124 against 20,667) voted "yes." In Oregon, Republican Mark Hatfield, who spoke out against the war, was elected to the Senate.

Polls showed that Vietnam was uppermost in the minds of American voters. The Democrats lost forty-seven seats in the House of Representatives and three in the Senate because of disenchantment with President Johnson's war policy—but many voters elected "hawks," who favored a more vigorous pursuit of the war, rather than "doves," who wanted to end it. Faced with this setback, the Inter-University Committee concluded that more dramatic action was necessary. It decided to take the issue to the streets.

The professors, led by Douglas Dowd and Robert Greenblatt of Cornell and Sidney Peck of Case Western Reserve in Cleveland, had called representatives of traditional peace groups together to meet in Cleveland that summer. In the fall, the coalition was expanded to include a greater number of radical groups. Among the most active was the Socialist Workers Party and its young people's affiliate. Members of that group generally were referred to as "Trotskyists" because they were followers of Leon Trotsky, a Communist leader Stalin had expelled from the Soviet Union.

At Peck's suggestion, A. J. Muste was installed as chairman. The participants approved a program of "noncompliance" with the war outlined by one of Muste's associates, Sidney Lens, and proclaimed a new organization, the November 5–8 Mobilization Committee. On these dates in 1966 antiwar groups were expected to take whatever action fitted their local situation.

The November mobilizations were modest affairs. They included the usual demonstrations and vigils, as well as art fairs, distributing leaflets at military bases, and ringing of doorbells to meet people on a one-on-one basis. In New York City, twenty thousand citizens turned out for yet another demonstration. In Cleveland, twelve hundred people walked in a driving rain behind the famous pediatrician, Benjamin Spock. About a thousand marched in Detroit, despite a snowstorm and threats by a rightist group called Breakthrough. Generally, the actions drew fewer participants than the Second International Days of Protest.

However, 1967 brought a major increase in antiwar activity. The November 5–8 Mobilization Committee became the Spring Mobilization Committee, with plans for large demonstrations to be held on April 15 in New York City and San Francisco. At the University of Chicago, two hundred students met to establish a Student Mobilization Committee and plan for a national student strike in conjunction with the April 15 events.

Liberal opposition to the war was spurred by dispatches from Hanoi by Harrison Salisbury, a *New York Times* reporter, who disputed President Johnson's claim that only military targets were being hit in North Vietnam. About twenty-five hundred members of Women Strike for Peace marched at the Pentagon, insisting on carrying their protest to "the generals who send our sons to Vietnam." Large student demonstrations took place at sixty universities, protesting the draft and impeding job-recruiting by the Dow Chemical Company, which sold napalm to the American military. Hundreds were arrested. In February, more students were radicalized when *Ramparts* magazine published a sensational article reporting that the respected National Student Association had been secretly subsidized by the CIA since 1950.

Most important, perhaps, in mobilizing opposition to the war was the Reverend Martin Luther King, Jr., the nation's most respected civil rights leader, who spoke out openly against U.S. intervention in Vietnam. He accused the United States of being the "greatest purveyor of violence in the world today" and urged opposition to the war by people of all races. King was the main speaker at the Spring Mobilization in New York—this time to a crowd of two hundred to four hundred thousand. About seventy-five thousand demonstrated in San Francisco.

At the end of August, some three thousand opponents of the war gathered in Chicago to plan strategy for the 1968 presidential election. The Movement was gaining confidence and strength. Many participants favored a national ticket composed of King for president and Dr. Benjamin Spock for vice president. However, the National Conference for New Politics, as it was called, turned out to be deeply divided and, therefore, ineffective. It rejected the idea of an independent ticket by a weighted vote of 13,519 to 13,517, and went out of business shortly thereafter.

A move by more moderate elements to find a candidate to oppose Lyndon Johnson in 1968 was more successful. This effort, initiated by Allard Lowenstein, a former president of the National Student Association, fastened on Democratic Senator Eugene McCarthy of Minnesota as its presidential hopeful. McCarthy, like many moderates, opposed the war and favored a bombing halt and negotiations but stopped short of calling for the immediate withdrawal of U.S. troops from Vietnam. The McCarthy campaign was to play an important role in forcing Lyndon Johnson out of office.

After its April 1967 demonstrations, the Mobe underwent another change of name and elected a new steering committee. It was now called the National Committee to End the War in Vietnam, and it set the date for the next national action for October 21, 1967. There were two views of what form that action should take. One segment of the Mobe proposed another parade and rally in Washington, aiming at a gathering of one million demonstrators. If two hundred thousand or four hundred thousand could come out in New York, this new goal seemed within reach. But other delegates persuaded the Mobe to shift its strategy "from protest to resistance." They suggested an action to "confront the warmakers" at the Pentagon itself. Everyone knew, of course, that it would not be possible to seize the Pentagon, but the delegates believed that large-scale civil disobedience would dramatize growing public hostility toward the war.

The week before October 21 was designated as Stop the Draft Week; hundreds of draft cards were burned or turned back to the federal government on both coasts. In Washington, the day before the rallies, Dr. Benjamin Spock, the Reverend William Sloane Coffin, Jr., and others presented one thousand draft cards to the office of the U.S. attorney general.

The next day's rally began at the Lincoln Memorial, where more than a hundred thousand people marched and listened to speeches. From there the protesters headed across the Potomac River to the Pentagon. In the first row were noted author Norman Mailer, who later wrote a book about the event, *Armies of the Night*; poet Robert Lowell; author Dwight Macdonald; Monsignor Charles O. Rice, of Pittsburgh; Marcus Raskin, a former member of the National Security Council staff; Professor Noam Chomsky, of the Massachusetts Institute of Technology; and Sidney Lens.

By agreement with the government, the marchers were supposed to enter at a certain gate, but within a few minutes the fence around the Pentagon had been breached in three or four places. What was to have been a single march became a confused welter. Mailer was among the first arrested that day, but soon nearly a thousand others had been taken into custody as troops made sweeps across the mall. Many people were tear-gassed.

As darkness fell, dozens of small meetings were under way. Periodically the police or troops would attack and haul away a few prisoners. On the steps of the Pentagon, a phalanx of soldiers and demonstrators confronted each other. One of the march leaders took a bullhorn and made a one-minute speech, telling the troops that the war was not in their interest and urging them to "join us, join us." The speech was repeated every couple of minutes for an hour or more. It was later reported—though not fully confirmed—that a few soldiers did desert their ranks.

Long past midnight, the "confront the warmakers" demonstration came to an end. Undoubtedly, it had heartened many antiwar activists and disturbed millions of other Americans. But it did force the nation to confront, think about, and discuss the reality of the war—and, in the end, condemn it.

There were 448,000 U.S. troops on duty in Vietnam. Secretary of Defense Robert S. McNamara, one of the main architects of the war, was now urging President Johnson to scale down the conflict and accept a compromise settlement. Late in November, Johnson announced that McNamara would leave the cabinet to become president of the World Bank—an important step in the unraveling of the Johnson administration and its Vietnam policy.

7 THE BEGINNING OF THE END

"We begin '68 in a better position than we have ever been in before," a U.S. spokesman said at a press conference in Saigon on January 24, 1968. Most Americans still believed, at that point, that things were going fairly well in Vietnam. But a week later the roof fell in. At 3 A.M. on January 31—the Vietnamese New Year holiday, called Tet—nineteen Vietcong commandos shot their way into the American Embassy compound in Saigon, killing two military police. Only after six hours did the surprised American forces regain control of the embassy area.

That same morning, eighty-four thousand National Liberation Front (Vietcong) troops moved against five of the six largest cities in South Vietnam, thirty-six of its forty provincial capitals, and five dozen district capitals.

In Hue, Vietcong battalions, aided by regular North Vietnamese forces, brushed aside South Vietnamese troops and marched directly into the center of town to occupy the university, central market, and imperial citadel. In Saigon, parts of eleven Vietcong battalions moved into the grounds of the presidential palace, seized a government radio station, and fought their way into the Tonsonhut air base to blow up a number of planes. For two weeks, they held out in a section of the city called Cholon, sniping at South Vietnamese government forces.

At Khe Sanh, a remote mountain base in the north of the country, six thousand U.S. Marines were besieged for seventy-seven days by regular North Vietnamese troops. U.S. war planes dropped 220 thousand tons of TNT on the enemy in an effort to break the siege, but in vain. In the end, the base had to be evacuated, after 300 soldiers had been killed and 2,200 wounded. At one point, General Westmoreland formed a "small secret group" to consider a "nuclear defense of Khe Sanh."

Westmoreland and his team had once boasted that his intelligence was so thorough that "no Vietcong could cook a pot of rice undetected." But the Vietcong had smuggled thousands of weapons and many tons of ammunition behind American and ARVN lines (sometimes in funeral caskets or flower boxes) without being intercepted. "The plan of action—a simultaneous surprise attack on nearly every city, town and major military base throughout South Vietnam—was audacious in its conception and stunning in its implementation," wrote Don Oberdorfer of the *Washington Post*.

After the U.S. forces caught their breath, they reacted furiously to the attack, bombing and strafing cities that had not been touched before, destroying large segments of Kontum City, Can Tho, My Tho, Vinh Long, and above all, Hue. An American colonel, explaining why U.S. forces had shattered more than half of the village of Ben Tre, told an Associated Press reporter, "We had to destroy it in order to save it." After three weeks, the U.S. command placed the civilian toll at 165,000 and the figure for new refugees at two million. This did not include the casualties at Hue, where fighting was fiercest, or the fighting in the final weeks of the Tet offensive. U.S. losses in the two months of the offensive were 3,895 dead and about 10,000 wounded.

Afterward, General Westmoreland boasted that he had not been surprised by Tet—and that the enemy had, in fact, been defeated. But a secret report to President Johnson by General Earle G. Wheeler, the chairman of the Joint Chiefs of Staff, conceded that the enemy's "determination appears to be unshaken" and that the Vietcong was "operating with relative freedom in the countryside."

If the objective of the Vietcong offensive was to overthrow the South Vietnamese government and force U.S. troops to withdraw, it obviously had failed. But few people denied that the National Liberation Front had won a significant political victory. Almost no one had expected it to mount such a daring venture—to slip so many troops and so much war materiel behind the American lines and to fight in so many places at once.

Back home, some of America's most prestigious periodicals, including *Time*, *Life*, and *Newsweek*, expressed doubts for the first time about Johnson's Vietnam policy. The most popular television anchor, Walter Cronkite of CBS News, questioned whether the war could be won and predicted it would "end in a stalemate." Senator Eugene McCarthy's presidential campaign drew increasing attention and support. Senator Robert F. Kennedy asserted that the United States was not winning and should no longer really try; the game, he thought, was over. Before the month ended, General Westmoreland was recalled to Washington and appointed Army Chief of Staff—technically a promotion, but actually an acknowledgment that he had failed.

In mid-March, the results of the first presidential primary, in New Hampshire, carried an ominous message for President Johnson. Eugene McCarthy won 40 percent of the Democratic Party vote against the incumbent president— something unheard of in American politics. Furthermore, polls showed that Johnson's popularity was rapidly declining: By late March, only 36 percent of the American public still expressed confidence in the way he was handling the war. A distinguished group of "wise men"—former high officials, military officers, and other influential leaders—told the president it would take five to ten years to win the war. They urged him to cut his losses and get out.

In a televised announcement on March 31, Johnson said

he was ending the bombing of North Vietnam—except for an area in the southern panhandle—and then stunned the nation by saying, "I shall not seek, and I will not accept, the nomination of my party for another term as your president." The Vietnam War had ended Lyndon Johnson's political life.

In April, hundreds of thousands of college and high school students went "on strike" against the war. *The New York Times* estimated the number in New York alone at two hundred thousand. At Columbia University, students seized several buildings in protest against the war and the way that blacks in the neighborhood were being treated by the university. Other less dramatic demonstrations took place in scores of cities, drawing two hundred thousand to Central Park's Sheep Meadow in New York, with a turnout of thirty thousand in San Francisco and seven thousand in Chicago.

The Mobe's main target in 1968 was the Democratic Party's national convention, to be held that summer in Chicago. National Mobilization Committee leaders had expected Johnson to run for another term and assumed there would be a massive turnout of demonstrators at the convention. Among the ideas that had been under consideration were a "counterconvention" with its own delegates, speakers, and "nominees" from the peace movement. Another scenario, which had been suggested by Jerry Rubin and other radical Yippies—short for the Youth International Party—was a "funfest" that would draw half a million young people to Chicago to camp out, smoke pot, dance, and burn draft cards. Still another suggestion was to have had Senator McCarthy call a big rally of perhaps fifty to seventy-five thousand protesters at Soldiers Field.

All of these ideas had to be modified when President Johnson bowed out. Any demonstration in Chicago, it was assumed, now would be small and probably uneventful. As it turned out, the event *was* small; only about three thousand demonstrators came from out of town, and another nine thousand from Chicago itself. But it was not uneventful. Mayor Richard J. Daley turned what would otherwise have been a rout for the antiwar forces into a worldwide media sensation.

The mayor, an old-line urban machine boss accustomed to having his own way, rejected a request by Rennie Davis, coordinator of the event, that out-of-towners be allowed to sleep in the city parks. He also refused permits to march on State Street to the Grant Park band shell, or on Halsted Street to the Amphitheater where the convention would be held. Had Daley issued these permits, the antiwar protests would probably have taken place in an orderly and nonviolent fashion and would have drawn a small crowd and a few paragraphs in the press.

Instead, Daley mobilized approximately six thousand regular army troops, approximately five thousand members of the Illinois National Guard—all in full combat gear—and the entire local police force of twelve thousand, which was placed on twelve-hour shifts for the convention week, to contain an unarmed group of men, women, and children that never numbered more than twelve thousand. The city swarmed with tanks, armored cars, and National Guardsmen wearing gas masks. Soldiers were posted on the roof of the Field Museum, as if an outbreak of war was imminent.

The authorities were incapable of dealing with the Yippics' sense of fun. When the young protesters introduced a pig they had named Pigasus to the assembled press as their candidate for president and when they threatened to pour LSD into Lake Michigan, Daley and his police took them seriously. Arrests and beatings took place every night of the convention week. Even an all-out pacifist group led by Staughton Lynd and the Quakers was not permitted to walk on the sidewalk to the Amphitheater. According to a report prepared for the National Commission on the Causes and Prevention of Violence, sixty journalists who covered the parks and streets that week were injured, arrested, or had their equipment damaged by police. The report referred to the events of convention week as a "police riot."

On August 25, the day before the convention was to begin, the Yippies held a Festival of Life at Lincoln Park, about three miles north of the center of Chicago. At 11 P.M., police ordered the participants to leave and used tear gas, clubs, and unbridled brutality to enforce their order. Many innocent people blocks away were beaten by police, including a few who didn't even know a demonstration was under way.

The climax came on Wednesday, the day the Democrats were set to nominate their candidates. Some ten thousand antiwar protesters gathered at the Grant Park band shell to listen to speeches and music—a long, long way from the Amphitheater. Suddenly, two suspicious-looking young people pulled down the American flag flying from a flagpole. A Mobe leader threw her arms around the pole in a futile effort to prevent the two from raising a red shirt. The police started beating people at random. Rennie Davis, coordinator of the event, was battered so much that he required stitches in the head.

Meanwhile, at Dave Dellinger's suggestion, about three thousand people lined up on the sidewalk. They were prepared to walk peacefully to the Amphitheater and, if necessary, accept arrest. But as the marchers reached the Conrad Hilton, one of the main convention hotels, police shouting "Kill, kill, kill" charged the crowd with swinging clubs, battering hundreds of people, many of whom had nothing to do with the demonstration. Scores of journalists and television camera crews witnessed the scene. Hundreds of people required medical attention, and 660 demonstrators, including Yippie leader Jerry Rubin, were hauled off in paddy wagons. A number of convention delegates were among those chased into the hotel by the police and arrested there.

Later that evening two thousand people, including twenty-five convention delegates and some reporters, marched southward on the sidewalk, led by comedian Dick

Gregory, but they too were manhandled. About seventy-five were arrested.

Public reaction to the "police riot" was mixed. The liberal community was shocked by what had happened. Antiwar sentiment was now so strong that a convention resolution calling for a coalition government in South Vietnam and an end to the war lost by only a three-to-two-margin, though it represented stern criticism of the Democratic Party's own president, Lyndon Johnson. Conservatives, persuaded by Mayor Daley's insistence that the police had been provoked, felt that the authorities had been justified. Many political analysts concluded, however, that the "police riot" cost the Democrats and their candidate, Vice President Hubert Humphrey, the election.

The aftermath of the 1968 Chicago events caused as much of a sensation as the events themselves. In mid-March 1969, the U.S. Department of Justice secured indictments against eight individuals under a new law that had been enacted in 1968. Dave Dellinger, Rennie Davis, Tom Hayden, Jerry Rubin, Abbie Hoffman, Bobby Seale of the Black Panther Party, John Froines, and Lee Weiner, who became known in the press as the Conspiracy Eight, were charged with "traveling in interstate commerce to incite a riot." If convicted, they would be subject to sentences of five years on each of two counts. How the eight were selected was something of a mystery. For instance, neither Bobby Seale nor the Black Panther Party, a radical political organization oriented toward addressing black social issues, had played any role in the August events. Froines and Weiner were unknown and also had played no part in planning or executing the demonstrations.

The Chicago trial opened in September 1969 and continued for five explosive months. Judge Julius Hoffman refused to postpone the case so that Seale's attorney could undergo a scheduled gallbladder operation; he also refused to allow Seale to represent himself. In the ensuing shouting match between defendants and the judge, Seale was ordered bound and gagged. The situation became so unruly that Seale was severed from the case—and then freed in a separate trial.

The contest between the Chicago Eight (now Seven) and Judge Hoffman made headlines every day and was featured on the television news every evening. One day, Abbie Hoffman and Jerry Rubin appeared in court wearing judicial robes. One courtroom outburst followed another as the defendants charged the judge with prejudicial behavior. Judge Hoffman, in turn, not only revoked bail for some of the defendants—sending them to jail—but also issued 125 contempt citations at the end of the trial and sentenced the seven defendants and their two lawyers to a total of twelve years in jail.

The case itself ended in conviction of five of the defendants on just one count, but even that was overturned on appeal. So were the vast majority of the contempt-of-court citations; and for those that were upheld, the jail sentences were suspended.

Inevitably, Vietnam became the major issue of the 1968 election campaign, commanding even more attention than in 1964. Though some Americans still hoped for a military victory, most were simply tired of the war, its cost in human life, its seeming endlessness, and the disruption it was causing at home. Vice President Hubert Humphrey, the Democratic Party's presidential candidate, was handicapped by his close association with President Johnson's hard line. Humphrey tried to persuade Johnson to take a softer stance by ending air strikes against North Vietnam and turning over more responsibility for the war to the South Vietnamese regime. But Johnson was unyielding.

Only in September, toward the end of the election campaign, when it became apparent that Vietnam would ruin his prospects, did Humphrey publicly take a more moderate position. He called for a total bombing halt and "de-

Americanization" of the war. Finally, on October 31, just a few days before the voting, Johnson ordered the cessation of bombing.

Talks between the United States and North Vietnam, which had begun in Paris in mid-May, were enlarged to include both the South Vietnamese government and the National Liberation Front (Vietcong). But a silly dispute over the shape of the negotiating table held up the substantive talks until after the American presidential election. Humphrey made up a lot of ground in the last week or two of the campaign, but it was not enough. He finally lost by a margin of less than one percent to Richard Nixon, vice president in the Eisenhower years, who had been defeated by John F. Kennedy in 1960.

The Vietnam War did not pose the same problem for Nixon that it did for Humphrey. The Republicans had endorsed the war as strongly as the ruling party—but in the mind of the public it was the "Democrats' war." Nixon took advantage of that. Early in the election campaign, he let it be known that he had a "secret plan" to end the war, but could not disclose it until he became president because it might undercut Johnson's negotiations in Paris. The implication was that Nixon had a program for a quick settlement. In fact, however, Nixon's "secret plan"—as he and his chief aide, H. R. Haldeman, revealed many years later in their respective memoirs—was to bring North Vietnam to its knees by threatening to use nuclear weapons.

According to Haldeman, Nixon expected "to end it in his first year." Haldeman quoted Nixon as saying, "I call it the Madman Theory, Bob. I want the North Vietnamese to believe I've reached the point where I might do anything to stop the war. We'll just slip the word to them that 'for God's sake, you know Nixon is obsessed about communism. We can't restrain him when he's angry—and he has his hand on the nuclear button.' "

The situation looked favorable for Nixon in the first few

months of his term. The American people were willing to give him some time to bring about the peace he had promised—even though they had no idea what his plan was. They had never heard of the Madman Theory, or "Vietnamization," or any other specific plan, but they were willing to take the new president at his word that he meant to end the war soon.

"I decided," Nixon wrote in his memoirs, "to set November 1, 1969—the anniversary of Johnson's bombing halt—as the deadline for what would in effect be an ultimatum to North Vietnam." According to one senior official who worked with the National Security Council, at least three sites were selected as nuclear targets. The Vietnamese, however, refused to budge—and within the United States the antiwar movement brought into the streets on October 15 and November 15, 1969, the two largest groups of antiwar protesters in American history.

In his memoirs, Nixon noted that "the only chance for an ultimatum to succeed was to convince the Communists that I could depend on solid support at home . . . but the chances I would actually have that support were becoming increasingly slim."

8 A NEW BEGINNING?

President Nixon's principal deputy in carrying out his policy would be Professor Henry A. Kissinger, a Harvard political scientist well known in the academic world and among foreign policy experts as a scholar on international relations. For several years, Kissinger had been active behind the scenes in trying to start negotiations with the North Vietnamese to settle the war. Using his wide circle of friends and associates around the world, he attempted to bring Lyndon Johnson and Ho Chi Minh, or their representatives, together. The attempts established him as a man who, given the choice, favored a negotiated settlement of the war over a prolonged military effort to win it.

During the 1968 campaign, Kissinger had been a foreign policy adviser to New York Governor Nelson A. Rockefeller, who was an opponent of Nixon for the Republican presidential nomination. When Nixon defeated Rockefeller, Kissinger returned to Cambridge, Massachusetts, and wrote an article for the prestigious journal *Foreign Affairs* setting forth his views on how a negotiated settlement could be achieved. He had little hope then of being drafted for an important job in the Nixon administration.

The article was a realistic analysis of the Vietnam situation, as these excerpts show.

First, on strategy:

A guerrilla war differs from traditional military operation because its key prize is not control of territory but control of

---

the population. . . . Eighty percent of American forces came to be concentrated in areas containing less than four percent of the population; the locale of military operations was geographically removed from that of the guerrilla conflict. . . . The American strategy produced what came to be the characteristic feature of the Vietnam War: military successes that could not be translated into permanent political advantage. . . . As a result the American concept of security came to have little in common with the experience of the Vietnamese villagers.

On seeking a negotiated end to the war:

Our diplomacy and our strategy were conducted in isolation from each other. . . . Short of a complete collapse of our opponent, our military deployment was not well designed to support negotiations. For purposes of negotiating, we would have been better off with 100 percent control over 60 percent of the country than with 60 percent control over 100 percent of the country.

On the meaning of the Tet offensive:

In a guerrilla war, purely military considerations are not decisive: psychological and political factors loom at least as large. On that level the Tet offensive was a political defeat in the countryside for Saigon and the United States.

Kissinger's article then went on to point out that the United States could have little real control over the ultimate outcome in South Vietnam. The best Washington could hope for, he suggested, was negotiations that would guarantee a face-saving withdrawal for American troops and creation of conditions under which the Thieu government in Saigon and the opposition National Liberation Front could peacefully settle their differences. Such a settlement, in the Kissinger formula, would have been guaranteed by an international conference that would meet at the same time with a conference of negotiators from the United States, North Vietnam, the Saigon government, and the NLF.

As Kissinger expressed it:

The limits of the American commitment can be expressed in two propositions: First, the United States cannot accept a military defeat, or a change in the political structure of South Vietnam brought about by external military force; second, once North Vietnamese forces and pressures are removed, *the United States has no obligation to maintain a government in Saigon by force.* [Author's emphasis.]

When he wrote those words, Henry Kissinger was a forty-five-year-old professor on the fringes of power. He completed the manuscript before Nixon's election. A month after the election, he was summoned to Nixon's transition headquarters to be named the president's assistant for national security affairs. A few days after his appointment, Kissinger told a reporter about the forthcoming article, explaining it was his view of how the war could be settled and indicating it was to become the Nixon administration's view.

So the scene apparently was set in January 1969 for a quick end to the war, which had already claimed thirty thousand American lives, most of them in the preceding four years. A new president was in the White House, ready to implement his as yet undisclosed plan. He could preside over the liquidation of a war that was not of his making. He had an intellectually strong assistant who had already published his own plan.

In the early days of the new administration, Kissinger, showing a sure sense for public relations and personal promotion, dined with journalists, government officials, and other opinion-makers in Washington, telling them all they would see a Vietnam settlement by the fall of 1969.

Nixon's defense secretary, Melvin Laird, who as a Republican Congressman had accused Johnson of concealing the true costs of the war, began talking about "Vietnamization"—a process by which the Saigon government would be able to defend itself so that a systematic withdrawal of American troops could begin. The president himself called for simultaneous withdrawal of American and North Vietnamese troops.

On the surface, at least, it was all following the script Kissinger had laid down in *Foreign Affairs*. An air of optimism and good feeling swept the capital. But the quick settlement was not to be. Instead, Southeast Asia would suffer six more years of continued and widened warfare in which almost as many Americans lost their lives as had before Nixon took office.

From the beginning, the Nixon administration's Vietnam policies suffered from the same split focus that had bedeviled the now-departed President Johnson. Outwardly, the Paris negotiations, which now included, reluctantly, representatives of the Saigon government and, more eagerly, the Vietcong, were encouraged. In June 1969, Nixon traveled to Midway Island in the Pacific to confer with Thieu and announce the withdrawal of twenty-five thousand American troops from Vietnam. Observers thought they were beginning to see some of the long-promised light at the end of the tunnel.

A report in the *New York Times* from Midway pointing out differences between the Johnson and Nixon styles was indicative:

> To an extent, the differences between Mr. Johnson's trips and that currently undertaken by Mr. Nixon spring from the changing nature of the war in Vietnam and the changing nature of the American commitment. The bullish predictions of military victory that characterized Mr. Johnson's sessions in Honolulu and Manila three years ago have been replaced by more modest and conditional rhetoric. The conversation now deals with supervised elections, with the subtleties of negotiating tactics in Paris, and with limited troop withdrawals. And, as the substance of these conferences has changed, so has the mood and tone.

But unknown to the journalists, the Nixon administration had already begun to repeat the mistakes of its predecessor. Nixon had secretly authorized the bombing of Cambodia in a futile attempt to stop the movement of supplies through the jungles of that peaceful country, which was trying to maintain its neutrality while powerful forces battled each other just across the frontier.

One year later, the bombing having failed, Cambodia was invaded by American troops in search of the enemy command centers and supply depots from which the war in South Vietnam was allegedly directed and supported. Cambodia was sucked into the whirlpool of violence and killing.

The invasion of Cambodia exposed the intentions and tactics of the Nixon administration. Though thousands of American troops had been sent across the border, the administration refused to call it an invasion; the word *incursion* was used. The U.S. forces went in search of what was described as COSVN, the Central Office for South Vietnam. To hear government briefers talk about it was to picture a huge Pentagon in the jungles, but the most the invaders found was a group of abandoned little huts. Despite Kissinger's 1969 article, the Nixon administration had clearly decided to use American troops in sparsely populated territory.

The protest movement that was so alive in Chicago in 1968 continued in 1969 and the first half of 1970. Huge demonstrations took place in Washington in October and November 1969. Young antiwar protesters with their long hair and unconventional dress were joined in the streets by large numbers of their more sedate parents. Now, in the aftermath of the Cambodian invasion, a new spasm of protest erupted in the United States, particularly on university campuses.

On May 4, 1970, a group of students at Kent State University in eastern Ohio staged a protest near their campus ROTC armory. The National Guard had been called out to preserve order, and in a moment of panic the guardsmen opened fire on the students and four were killed. Within days more than four hundred colleges and universities throughout the country shut down in protest. Tens of thousands of demonstrators ringed the White House in a candlelight march. The capital was jammed with protesters vowing to shut down the United States government. Thousands were arrested and held in makeshift detention centers in actions that would later be judged illegal.

Kissinger's support among intellectuals had all but evaporated. A group of his former Harvard colleagues wrote to him in protest. Four of his White House staff members resigned. When Stuart H. Loory, a *Los Angeles Times* reporter, wrote that the "patina is beginning to wear off the Kissinger mystique," the presidential adviser tried to have Loory expelled from the White House. By late summer, former Pennsylvania Governor William Scranton, appointed to head a commission to investigate campus protests, reported that the war must be ended to heal what the commission called the greatest division in American society since the Civil War.

In 1968, before he left the Johnson administration, Defense Secretary Robert S. McNamara ordered a top-secret study of the Vietnam War designed to compile in one place the documents from which judgments could be made about what had gone wrong. The study was photocopied and leaked to the *New York Times*, which began publishing excerpts on June 19, 1971.

The collection was dubbed the Pentagon Papers. The government went to court and forced the *New York Times* to suspend publication, despite the First Amendment to the Constitution which prohibits prior censorship. A selection from the papers showed up in the *Washington Post*. It, too, was shut off. Other excerpts appeared in the *St. Louis Post Dispatch*, the *Boston Globe*, and the *Los Angeles Times*.

It was intellectual guerrilla warfare orchestrated by Daniel Ellsberg, then forty years old, who had once been a Pentagon official, a gun-toting supporter of the Vietnam effort, and for a short time even a consultant to Kissinger. Now he had released the Pentagon study in an effort to expose the meaning of the war to all. Though by no means a complete record, the papers showed how the United States had bungled into the war by holding an unfounded impression of its own power, by misunderstanding the Communist threat worldwide, and by having a mistaken view of its ability to influence the people and leadership of South Vietnam and of how to use diplomacy to settle the war.

Though the documents dated back to the Eisenhower, Kennedy, and Johnson administrations, the Nixon administration was furious over the release. Its attempts at censorship ended when the Supreme Court ruled in favor of the newspapers' right to publish. Defeated in this attempt to impose prior censorship of the press for the first time in the peacetime history of the nation, the administration mounted a vigorous campaign to suppress civil rights and individual freedom in this country by illegal means.

Within a month after publication of the Pentagon Papers, White House domestic affairs chief John Erlichman had formed a group called "the plumbers" to investigate Ellsberg, by then identified as the man who had given the papers to the press. The plumbers broke into the offices of Ellsberg's psychiatrist to try to find incriminating evidence against him many months before the more famous break-in at the Democratic National Headquarters at the Watergate office building in Washington.

The administration was conducting illegal wiretaps of officials and journalists, some authorized by Kissinger himself. The FBI and the Internal Revenue Service were being encouraged to harass those thought to be enemies of the administration and critics of its policies. Within the White House, actual lists of "enemies" were compiled.

Coverup had become the chief tactic of the administration months before the coverup of President Nixon's involvement in the Watergate break-in was undertaken. The Nixon administration had been hiding from the American public the true nature of its efforts in Vietnam. Kissinger himself had begun negotiations with the North Vietnamese, which he kept secret from the Saigon regime.

As 1971 came to a close, American troop strength in South Vietnam, which had reached more than 540,000 men in 1968, had shrunk to 140,000.

In Paris, the negotiations begun during the Johnson administration three years before droned onward. The question of the table shape was long since settled, so the four participants met regularly. But these negotiations were only a cover; Kissinger had opened his own secret channel to the North Vietnamese. In February 1970, he met for the first time with Le Duc Tho, the North Vietnamese Communist official responsible for operations in South Vietnam. This was the first of the discussions that would lead, over three years, to U.S. withdrawal from the war. Although Kissinger told Thieu, the South Vietnamese president, about those secret talks, he misled him about their purpose, which would leave the Saigon government on its own when the United States withdrew.

In 1979, Thieu would tell the German news magazine *Der Spiegel*, "What he [Kissinger] and the U.S. Government exactly wanted was to withdraw as fast as possible, to secure the release of U.S. prisoners. They said they wanted an honorable solution, but really they wanted to wash their hands of the whole business and scuttle and run. . . . They did not want to be accused of abandoning us. That was the difficulty."

For a generation, the rationale behind the American support of the anti-Communist forces in Southeast Asia had been that the movement led by Ho Chi Minh was nothing more than a front for the expansion of international communism. At times, the assumption was that international communism was directed by the Soviet leadership in Moscow; at times the accusation was that it was led by the Chinese from Beijing; and sometimes both were seen as having a hand in the leadership.

By the beginning of 1972, Kissinger had laid the diplomatic groundwork for Nixon to visit both Moscow and Beijing. The American administration was willing to negotiate with its powerful enemies while continuing to exert military pressure against a weaker one.

In February 1972, President Nixon, whose early career was based in large part on opposition to the Chinese Communists, arrived in Beijing on a state visit to improve relations with the People's Republic of China. In May, Nixon traveled to Moscow to repair relations with the leadership in the Kremlin. Meanwhile, in a fit of despair over the slow pace of negotiations with Hanoi and the stepped-up North Vietnamese military actions, he had authorized the bombing of an area near Hanoi and Haiphong as well as the mining of Haiphong harbor.

Shortly after Nixon's return from Moscow, five men were arrested while trying to burglarize the Democratic National headquarters in the Watergate. The events that would finally force Nixon to become the first man in history to resign the presidency were set in motion. By mid-1972, Nixon and his assistants no longer saw the Hanoi regime, the Chinese Communists, or the Kremlin leadership as real enemies. They were negotiating with the Communists.

They were, however, waging unconditional war on Congressional leaders who were bent on restraining the use of military power in Southeast Asia, journalists who were working hard to dig out the details of the administration's deceit and illegalities, the American people, who were opposing the war in growing numbers, the Saigon regime, which was battling for survival, and many leaders of nations allied with the United States who saw this country as a military giant out of control.

Nixon's opponent in the 1972 presidential election campaign was Senator George McGovern of South Dakota, a decorated World War II bomber pilot with a record of vigorous opposition to the Vietnam War. McGovern's campaign for the nomination had been unconventional, involving a massive reform of Democratic Party rules to seat the delegates who would nominate him at the political convention. Nixon's campaign was relentless; in the election, he buried McGovern in the heaviest electoral landslide ever. Nonetheless, Nixon felt threatened. The atmosphere in Washington, so hopeful three years before, was now beclouded with mistrust and deceit.

A month before the election, Kissinger and Le Duc Tho of North Vietnam reached an agreement in Paris on withdrawal of the last American forces. The White House had trouble selling that agreement to the Thieu regime, in Saigon. Under great pressure to go along, Thieu came up with dozens of proposed changes in the agreement. To put pressure on Nixon North Vietnam then released details of the original agreement, which showed how the current agreement met all American demands. Kissinger reacted to the release of the details by claiming "peace is at hand" if only the North Vietnamese would accept some of the seemingly minor changes in the agreement. They would not.

So, after the election, Nixon authorized the so-called Christmas bombing of the area around Hanoi and Haiphong, an eleven-day rain of bombs that devastated large areas of Hanoi and Haiphong and resulted in the shooting down of twenty-three American planes. The bombing stopped on December 30, after the North Vietnamese said they would resume negotiations. In January, a peace agreement was finally signed in Paris.

The agreement called for an internationally supervised cease-fire, a full accounting of all American prisoners of war and their release within sixty days, the withdrawal of all American forces within that same time period, and a statement that the people of South Vietnam would be guaranteed the right to their own future without outside interference.

Nixon announced all this in a televised speech, saying the United States had achieved "peace with honor."

In fact, the details of the settlement were almost identical to the agreement Kissinger and Le Duc Tho had reached three months before. And it followed all of the precepts Kissinger had laid down in his January 1969 article in *Foreign Affairs*. The sad fact was that the United States and North Vietnam reached an agreement in 1973 that could have been negotiated in 1969.

On March 29, the sixty-day withdrawal period came to an end. At the time, the government reported that the last of 589 prisoners of war had gained their release and the last American troops were evacuated from South Vietnam. But it was already apparent that the agreement was nothing more than a piece of paper that allowed the United States to make a more or less graceful exit from Vietnam. "The cease-fire isn't working," one "highly placed diplomat" told the *New York Times* in March of 1973. Two years later, in the spring of 1975, the North Vietnamese overran the South. The United States did nothing to stop that. It had grown preoccupied with its own domestic crisis—the discovery of the extent to which the Nixon administration, with the president's support, had violated the Constitution of the United States.

In July 1974, the Judiciary Committee of the House of Representatives recommended the impeachment of the president, having established that he was deeply involved in covering up the Watergate burglaries and everything associated with them. Nixon resigned his office in August 1974.

Less than a year earlier Vice President Spiro T. Agnew had resigned after his criminal activities as governor of Maryland were discovered. Both the president and vice president stood accused of crimes that forced them out of office. Nixon was replaced by Vice President Gerald R. Ford, who had taken that job when Agnew resigned. Within a month, Ford had pardoned Nixon for any crimes, even before the former president was formally charged and tried.

In January 1975, the North Vietnamese began an offensive that was successful even beyond their expectations. In the past, American troops and airpower would have intervened.

But the South Vietnamese army, now left to its own devices, disintegrated. By mid-April, the North Vietnamese were at the gates to Saigon. On April 21, Thieu resigned and left the country. Kissinger was quoted as opposing an evacuation by American civilians in the city. He even banned the use of the word *evacuation* in any American government statement.

But the evacuation was inevitable and came quickly. On April 29, the last Americans and many Vietnamese considered to be under severe threat, were lifted by helicopter from the roof of the American Embassy in Saigon. The war was over.

President Ford tried to put it all behind with a brief statement that ended: "This action closes a chapter in the American experience. I ask all Americans to close ranks, to avoid recrimination about the past, to look ahead to the many goals we share and to work together on the great tasks that remain to be accomplished."

Quick attempts to bind up the wounds could go only so far. Ford had granted an amnesty to draft evaders, but not all took advantage of it. The military draft had been abolished and was replaced by an all-volunteer army. That had muted the demonstrations by young people, but their disaffection remained. The nation's drug problem had been intensified by the habits carried home from the war zones by tens of thousands of young Americans.

Some of them had been taught that brutality and the laws of survival in the jungle formed an acceptable code of conduct, and they brought that code home to everyday life. War breeds atrocity, but seldom, if ever, before had there been an American-perpetrated atrocity like the massacre of 347 Vietnamese, virtually all of them old men, women, and children, in the Vietnamese village of My Lai in March 1968. Lying and cheating among leadership, always in danger of going unpunished, became an even more acceptable standard not only in government but also in business where, in the late 1970s and 1980s, "yuppies" would count success as a goal, with little or no concern for moral or ethical standards.

This was the first war in which television cameras were almost everywhere, recording images of death and violence and bringing them home to living rooms with a speed never before contemplated. The impact that process had on the public—and on the mass media—has never been fully resolved.

The men who prolonged the Vietnam War would never come to terms truthfully with their own involvement, much less with other issues. In 1980, Henry Kissinger, stung by the criticism voiced by former President Thieu, was still justifying his own deviousness: "I continue to believe that the balance of forces . . . could have been maintained if Watergate had not destroyed our ability to obtain sufficient aid . . . from the Congress in 1973 and 1974. Had we known in 1972 what was to come in America, we would not have proceeded as we did."

The fact is that Henry Kissinger knew in 1969 what could be achieved in Vietnam. But he abandoned his beliefs, allowing hundreds of thousands of Americans, Vietnamese, Cambodians, Laotians, and others to be maimed and killed needlessly so that a so-called great power could save face.

Kissinger was not alone in allowing expediency to triumph over principle and even over realism when it came to formulating and carrying out American policy. However, the important question is not what the policymakers learned from the experience of Vietnam, but what the rest of us have learned.

SOURCES

Chapter 1

Halstead, Fred. *Out Now!* New York: Monad Press, 1978.
Newsweek, May 5, 1975, pp. 21–31; and May 12, 1975, pp. 26–29.

Chapter 2

Fall, Bernard B. *The Two Viet-Nams.* New York: Frederick A. Praeger, 1965.
Fitzgerald, Frances. *Fire in the Lake: The Vietnamese and the Americans in Vietnam.* Boston: Atlantic Monthly Press, 1972.
Gettleman, Marvin E., ed. *Vietnam: History, Documents, and Opinions of a Major World Crisis.* Greenwich, Conn.: Fawcett Publications, 1965.
Gettleman, Marvin E.; Franklin, Jane; Young, Marilyn; and Franklin, H. Bruce, eds. *Vietnam and America: A Documented History.* New York: Grove Press, 1985.
Goldman, Eric. *The Tragedy of Lyndon Johnson.* New York: Alfred A. Knopf, 1969.
Halstead, Fred. *Out Now!*
Information Please, 1982, pp. 399–400.
Lens, Sidney. *The Forging of the American Empire.* New York: Crowell, 1971.
Loory, Stuart H. *Defeated: Inside America's Military Machine.* New York: Random House, 1973.
The Pentagon Papers: The Secret History of the Vietnam War. New York: Bantam, 1971.
Schoenbrun, David. *Vietnam: How We Got In, How to Get Out.* New York: Atheneum, 1968.
Zinn, Howard. *A People's History of the United States.* New York: Harper & Row, 1980.

Chapter 3

Congressional Record of the Senate. May 9, 1967.

Effros, William G., compiler. *Vietnam 1945–1970*. New York: Random House, 1970.

Fitzgerald, Frances. *Fire in the Lake*.

Gettleman, Marvin E., et al. *Vietnam and America*.

Goldman, Eric. *The Tragedy of Lyndon Johnson*.

Halstead, Fred. *Out Now!*

Hilsman, Roger. *To Move a Nation*. New York: Delta, 1967.

Lens, Sidney. *The Military-Industrial Complex*. Princeton, N.J.: Pilgrim Press, 1970.

Maclear, Michael. *The Ten Thousand Day War: Vietnam 1945–75*. New York: Avon, 1981.

The Pentagon Papers.

Powers, Thomas. *The War at Home*. New York: Grossman Publishers, 1973.

Stavins, Ralph; Barnet, Richard J.; Raskin, Marcus G. *Washington Plans an Aggressive War*. New York: Vintage, 1971.

Wise, David. *The American Police State*. New York: Random House, 1976.

Wise, David, and Ross, Thomas B. *The Invisible Government*. New York: Random House, 1964.

Wise, David. *The Politics of Lying*. New York: Random House, 1973.

Zaroulis, Nancy, and Sullivan, Gerald. *Who Spoke Up? American Protest Against the War in Vietnam 1963–1975*. Garden City, N.Y.: Doubleday, 1984.

Zinn, Howard. *A People's History of the United States*.

Chapter 4

Boettcher, Thomas D. *Vietnam: The Valor and the Sorrow*. Boston: Little, Brown, 1985.

Committee of Concerned Asian Scholars. *The Indochina Story*. New York: Bantam, 1970.

Kahin, George McTurnan, and Lewis, John W. *The United States in Vietnam*. New York: Delta, 1967.

Karnow, Stanley. *Vietnam: A History*. New York: Penguin, 1984.

Maclear, Michael. *The Ten Thousand Day War: Vietnam 1945–75*.

The Pentagon Papers.

Pickerell, James. *Vietnam in the Mud*. New York: Bobbs-Merrill, 1966.

Stavins, Ralph, et al. *Washington Plans an Aggressive War*.

Zaroulis, Nancy, and Sullivan, Gerald. *Who Spoke Up?*
Zinn, Howard. *A People's History of the United States.*

Chapter 5

Committee of Concerned Asian Scholars. *The Indochina Story.*
Gettleman, Marvin, et al. *Vietnam and America.*
Halstead, Fred. *Out Now!*
Jacobs, Paul, and Landau, Saul. *The New Radicals.* New York: Vintage, 1966.
Lens, Sidney. *The Bomb.* New York: Lodestar Books, 1982.
————. *The Forging of the American Empire.*
————. *Unrepentant Radical.* Boston: Beacon Press, 1980.
Powers, Thomas. *The War at Home.*
Sale, Kirkpatrick. *SDS.* New York: Vintage, 1974.
Skolnick, Jerome H. *The Politics of Protest.* New York: Clarion/Simon & Schuster, 1969.
Viorst, Milton. *Fire in the Streets: America in the 1960's.* New York: Simon & Schuster, 1979.
Zaroulis, Nancy, and Sullivan, Gerald. *Who Spoke Up?*

Chapter 6

Boettcher, Thomas D. *Vietnam: The Valor and the Sorrow.*
Committee of Concerned Asian Scholars. *The Indochina Story.*
Fitzgerald, Frances. *Fire in the Lake.*
Halstead, Fred. *Out Now!*
Kahin, George McTurnan, and Lewis, John W. *The United States in Vietnam.*
Karnow, Stanley. *Vietnam: A History.*
Lens, Sidney. *Unrepentant Radical.*
Maclear, Michael. *The Ten Thousand Day War: Vietnam 1945–75.*
The Pentagon Papers.
Zaroulis, Nancy, and Sullivan, Gerald. *Who Spoke Up?*

Chapter 7

Burchett, Wilfred G. *Grasshoppers and Elephants: Why Vietnam Fell.* New York: Urizen Books, 1977.
Fitzgerald, Frances. *Fire in the Lake.*
Halstead, Fred. *Out Now!*
Lens, Sidney. *The Day Before Doomsday.* Garden City, N.Y.: Doubleday, 1977.

_____. *Unrepentant Radical.*
The Pentagon Papers.
Zaroulis, Nancy, and Sullivan, Gerald. *Who Spoke Up?*

Chapter 8

Ellsberg, Daniel. *Papers on the War.* New York: Simon & Schuster, 1972.
Kaplan, H. J. "Remembering Vietnam." *Commentary* 84, no. 6, December 1987.
Karnow, Stanley. *Vietnam: A History.*
Kissinger, Henry A. "The Viet Nam Negotiations." *Foreign Affairs,* 47, no. 2, January 1969.
Lens, Sidney. *Unrepentant Radical.*
Loory, Stuart H., and Kraslow, David. *The Secret Search for Peace in Vietnam.* New York: Random House, 1968.
The *Los Angeles Times,* July 5, 1970, p. 1.
The *New York Times,* June 9, 1969, p. 16; January 24, 1973, p. 1; March 29, 1973, p. 1; January 7, 1975, p. 1; April 22, 1975, p. 1; April 30, 1975, p. 17.
"U.S. Casualties in Southeast Asia." Washington, D.C.: U.S. Government Printing Office, November 11, 1986.

ADDITIONAL SUGGESTED READING

Archer, Jules. *The Incredible Sixties: The Stormy Years That Changed America*. San Diego, CA: Harcourt, Brace, Jovanovich, 1986.

Ashabranner, Brent. *Always to Remember: The Story of the Vietnam Veteran's Memorial*. New York: Dodd, Mead, 1988.

Bonds, Ray, ed. *The Vietnam War: The Illustrated History of the Conflict in Southeast Asia*. New York: Crown, 1983.

Currey, Richard. *Fatal Light*. New York: E.P. Dutton/Seymour Lawrence, 1988. (adult fiction)

Dolan, Edward F. *MIA: Missing in Action: A Vietnam Drama*. New York: Watts, 1989.

Haskins, James, and Benson, Kathleen. *The 60s Reader*. New York: Viking Kestrel, 1988.

Jensen, Kathryn. *Pocket Change*. New York: Macmillan, 1989. (fiction)

Lawson, Don. *An Album of the Vietnam War*. New York: Franklin Watts, 1986.

_____. *The United States in the Vietnam War*. New York: Harper, 1981.

Mabie, Margot C. *Vietnam There & Here*. New York: Holt, 1985.

Mason, Bobbie Ann. *In Country*. New York: Harper, 1985. (adult fiction)

Myers, Walter Dean. *Fallen Angels*. New York: Scholastic, 1988. (fiction)

Wolitzer, Meg. *Caribou*. New York: Greenwillow, 1984. (fiction)

Wright, David K. *War in Vietnam, Book I: Eve of Battle; War in Vietnam, Book II: A Wider War; War in Vietnam, Book III: Victimization; War in Vietnam, Book IV: Fall of Vietnam*. Chicago: Children's Press, 1989.

INDEX

Page numbers in *italics* refer to illustrations.

fought France and Japan, 6
guerrilla war, 91–92

Haiphong, 8, 11, 56, 99–100
Haldeman, H.R., 89
Ham Rong Bridge, 26, 33
Hanoi, 7, 11, 26, 56, 62, 77,
   99–100
Hatfield, Mark, 76
"hawks," 34, 48, 76
Hayden, Tom, 42, 45, 52, 87
Herrick, Commodore John J.,
   21
Ho Chi Minh, 6–7, 9, 22, 24,
   26, 56, 91, 98
Ho Chi Minh Trail, 42, 56
Hoffman, Abbie, 87–88
Hoffman, Judge Julius, 87–88
Hue, 14, 61, 81–82
Humphrey, Hubert, 87–89

Ia Drang River, 38–39
Illinois National Guard, 85
impeachment, 101
   1974 rally, 74
Inter-University Committee for
   Debate on Foreign Policy,
   75–76

Johnson, Lyndon B., 9, 19–21,
   24–26, 27, 33–35, 40,
   46–48, 51, 55–57, 61–64,
   66, 76–78, 80, 82–84,
   90–91, 93–94
   administration, 22, 35, 53,
   57, 61, 80, 96–98

Karnow, Stanley, 38–39
Kennedy, John F., 8, 11, 23,
   55, 63, 89
   administration, 15
Kennedy, Robert F., 63, 83
Kent State University, 95

Khe Sanh, 34, 81–82
King, Reverend Martin Luther,
   Jr., 43, 49, 67, 77–78
Kissinger, Henry, 91–94, 96–
   98, 100–103
Ky, see Nguyen Cao Ky

Laird, Melvin, 93
Laos, 4, 10–11, 20, 42, 56–57
   Laotian casualties, 103
League for the Independence
   of Vietnam, see Vietminh
Le Duc Tho, 98, 100–101
Lens, Sidney, 42, 52, 70, 76, 79
Liberation, 41–42
Life, 18, 50, 83
Lippmann, Walter, 63–64
Look, 19
Loory, Stuart H., 96
Los Angeles Times, 96
Lowenstein, Allard, 78
Lynd, Staughton, 42, 48, 50,
   52, 66, 85

MacArthur, General Douglas, 7
Maddox, 20–22
Madman Theory, 89–90
Mailer, Norman, 49, 79
Mansfield, Mike, 11
McCarthy, Eugene, 78, 84
   presidential campaign, 83
McGovern, George, 99
McNamara, Robert S., 16, 25,
   40, 50, 55, 80, 96
Mekong Delta, 10–11, 34
Morgenthau, Hans J., 49
Morse, Wayne, 22, 63
Muste, Reverend A.J., 41, 49–
   50, 52, 63, 66, 76
My Lai, 102

napalm, 26, 38, 41, 46, 58, 66,
   77
   napalm bombs, 28

SANE, *see* Committee for a Sane Nuclear Policy

San Francisco, 42, 44, 65, 77–78, 84

Scheer, Robert, 49, 75

"seal and search," 39

Seale, Bobby, 87–88

"search and destroy missions," *32*, 37–39, 57

Second International Days of Protest, March 1966, 64, 77

South Vietnam, 1–2, 15–16, 18–19, 22, 34–35, 53, 57, 61–63, 81–82, 92, 97–98
army, 37, 40, 59, 81, 102
government, 24, 35–36, 40, 59–61, 81, 83, 88, 94, 97–98, 100

Soviet Union, 33, 35, 76

Speak-out at the Pentagon, 49–50

Spock, Dr. Benjamin, 49, *69*, 77–79

Spring Mobilization Committee, 77

Stone, I. F., 20, 46, 48

Stop the Draft Week, 79

Strategic Hamlet Program, 14, 36

Students for a Democratic Society (SDS), 45–47

"teach-ins," 4, 46, 48–49, 63, 75

Tet, 81
Tet offensive, 58, 82, 92

Thieu, *see* Nguyen Van Thieu

Tonkin Gulf, 20–21

Tonkin Gulf Resolution, 22, 48, 62

United States, 1, 4, 6, 89, 92–93, 95–96
Constitution, 22, 96, 101
Department of Defense, 7, 17, 50
Department of Justice, 87
Joint Chiefs of Staff, 10, 26, 82–83
Marine Corps, 26, *28*, 38, 81
military, *29*, *30*, *32*, 37–39, 58, 93, 95, 98
National Security Council, 10, 90
peace talks, 89, 92, 94, 98, 100–101
Senate Foreign Relations Committee, 22, 62

Vietcong, 13–14, 16–19, 24–25, 33–40, 50, 58, 61, 81–83, 94

"Vietnamization," 90, 93

Vietminh, 6–7, 9–13

Vo Nguyen Giap, 8

Washington Post, 18, 82, 96

Watergate burglaries, 97, 99, 101, 103

Weiner, Lee, 87

Westmoreland, General William, 34–40, 57–59, 82–83

Women for Peace, 54

Women's International League for Peace and Justice, 44

Women Strike for Peace, 44, 52, 63, 77

Youth International Party (Yippies), 84–86

The late SIDNEY LENS was one of the leaders of the peace movement, co-chairing the New Mobilization Committees to End the War in Vietnam. He was also a co-founder of the Chicago Peace Council.

Mr. Lens wrote twenty-three books for young people and adults on foreign affairs, labor, communism, and the American Left. His previous books for Lodestar are *Strikemakers and Strikebreakers* and *The Bomb*, a *School Library Journal* Best Book of the Year and a Jane Addams Peace Award Honor Book.

Sidney Lens was a senior editor of the *Progressive* magazine and wrote articles for numerous newspapers and magazines, including the *Nation*, *Harvard Business Review*, the *Progressive*, the *Chicago Sun-Times*, and the *New York Times*.

STUART H. LOORY is vice-president of Cable News Network World Report and editor-in-chief of the CNN World Report. He has been managing editor of the *Chicago Sun-Times* and has held various staff positions with the *Los Angeles Times*, the *New York Times*, and the *New York Herald Tribune*. Mr. Loory's books include *Defeated: Inside America's Military Machine* and *The Secret Search for Peace in Vietnam*.

ERWIN KNOLL is the editor of the *Progressive*, a national magazine of investigative reporting, political analysis, and commentary, published in Madison, Wisconsin. He has been on the staff of the *Washington Post* and the Newhouse National News Service, covering the White House during the Johnson administration. Mr. Knoll is coauthor of *Anything But the Truth* and *Scandal in the Pentagon*, among other books.